A
BLOODHOUND
TO DIE FOR

**Center Point
Large Print**

**This Large Print Book carries the
Seal of Approval of N.A.V.H.**

A
BLOODHOUND
TO DIE FOR

Virginia Lanier

CENTER POINT PUBLISHING
THORNDIKE, MAINE

This book is for ShaRee Russo,
who anticipated my every need and performed miracles . . .

This Center Point Large Print edition
is published in the year 2004 by arrangement with
HarperCollins Publishers.

Copyright © 2003 by Virginia Lanier.

The text of this Large Print edition is unabridged. In other
aspects, this book may vary from the original edition. Printed in
Thailand. Set in 16-point Times New Roman type.

ISBN 1-58547-483-5

Library of Congress Cataloging-in-Publication Data

Lanier, Virginia, 1930-
   A bloodhound to die for / Virginia Lanier.--Center Point large print ed.
      p. cm.
   ISBN 1-58547-483-5 (lib. bdg. : alk. paper)
   1. Siddon, Jo Beth (Fictitious character)--Fiction. 2. Women dog owners--Fiction.
3. Bloodhound--Fiction. 4. Georgia--Fiction. 5. Large type books. I. Title.

PS3562.A524B57 2004
813'.54--dc22
                                                              2004005837

Dogs are not our whole life,
but they make our lives whole.
—ROGER CARAS

1

"Smile as You're Being Gutted"
August 23, Friday, 11:10 A.M.

Jasmine Jones halloed from the office and I yelled back that I was in the bedroom. When she entered, I held up a bra that had seen better days.

"Think this will last awhile longer?"

I had upended three drawers from my bureau, making a large messy pile in the middle of my bed. The empties were aligned alongside, waiting to be refilled with meticulously folded and correctly sorted bits of lingerie.

Jasmine fingered the frayed elastic straps and rubbed her long graceful fingers over the small safety pin that secured one strap I had failed to notice. I mentally braced for the lecture on slovenliness that was sure to come. She walked to my small wastebasket and dropped the bra inside without saying a word.

Returning to my side, she put her hands on her hips and studied my expression.

Jasmine is beautiful. Flawless skin a rich shade of chocolate, a regal Nefertiti neck, ebony hair, short and casually curled, and a slender body with all the curves in the right places.

My name is Jo Beth Sidden. Jasmine is my employee

and friend and lives just across the driveway in a garage apartment. I'm an inch taller at five-seven and always looked dumpy beside her until recently. The trauma of a murder trial coupled with having to turn my prize bloodhound Bobby Lee against me finally gave me the willowy silhouette I craved, but this still wasn't enough to make us equal. My mousy, medium-brown hair, short and impossibly curly from birth, and my pale complexion spattered with faint brown freckles across my nose just couldn't compete when in her presence.

"What happened this morning?" she demanded.

"Nothing much. Went shopping for some new clothes. All of you have been fussing at me to buy some new clothes for weeks. Since most of them have been altered to some degree, they make me look as if I'm wearing a croker sack. So I went to spend some serious money at Estelle's Boutique out in the South Gate Mall. At least that's where I was gonna start."

I saw her quick survey to see if she had missed a pile of plastic bags and candy-apple-red striped boxes.

"No, I didn't buy anything, because I was shown the front door and told to leave and to never, ever, return."

I heard her quick intake of breath and saw her bewilderment.

"Why?"

"You're aware that I know Balsa City citizens' genealogy better than most. I grew up here. Family connections take a lifetime to study and are taught to the young as if they are school lessons. I just didn't think. I'll know better next time. I completely forgot that

Estelle is married to my ex Bubba's second cousin, once removed."

"Second cousin, once removed?" she marveled. "Give me a break. I've never heard of such nonsense!"

"I'm surprised that you're surprised. You were raised here too. Doesn't the black community support its relatives the very same way?"

I knew better than to use the term *African American*. She gave me an acrimonious smile.

"Not exactly. Some of us go to great lengths to avoid, acknowledge, or even think about blood ties."

My gut clenched. I had struck a nerve. I found out last year purely by chance that Jasmine's mother was alive and well and resided less than four miles from here. She had never let her mother's name pass her lips. I had assumed incorrectly that she was dead.

I knew that Jasmine had worked the streets as a prostitute from the time she was twelve until she was nineteen. Hank Cribbs, now sheriff of Dunston County, was a lieutenant back then. He had arrested her and tried to get her off the streets many times before she changed her occupation. When I met her, she was running a small barbecue joint in Shantytown.

"God, I'm sorry, Jasmine. I spoke without thinking."

Her smile was fleeting. "I'm glad you didn't act as if you were unaware of my mother's existence. I know that Granny Rose would have mentioned my mother when you visited with her a while back. I kept waiting for you to ask me about her, but you never did."

"I was trying to be tactful, dammit, and I'll have to admit I was hurt that you hadn't confided in *me*. I thought we shared secrets. Granny Rose said that you would tell me about her when the time was right."

"I guess the time is right. I feel like telling you about her. Are you sure you want to hear this?"

"Absolutely. I'm all ears." I patted the side of the bed across from me and grabbed up the pile of lingerie, moving it between us. "We can sort and fold while we talk."

"First, I want to hear what Estelle said to you. Finish telling me what happened."

"I was in a dressing room getting ready to try on a couple of outfits when her salesperson informed her of my presence. Thank God I still had my own clothes on. She came in quickly and manhandled me out into the store, then gave me the bum's rush to the front door. I bet she would have done the same even if I had been in the altogether."

"You really think so?"

"You bet. All the way to the front door she was screaming at me that I had murdered a member of her family, she didn't need any of my blood money, and it made her ill just seeing me walking around free after a jury had found me guilty."

The member of her family was Bubba, who had beaten me up repeatedly during our ill-fated marriage, then stalked me mercilessly after our divorce.

"What did you do?" Jasmine's eyes were wide and expectant. She knew my usual response, because of my quick temper, would have been to mop up the floor with Estelle, while I was reading everyone within hearing range the riot act.

"I smiled, wished her a nice day, and came home."

Frowning, Jasmine leaned forward and placed her hand on my forehead.

"Do you feel feverish? Dizzy? You must be coming down with something."

"None of the above. I was simply trying to act mature and think before I leap."

"This doesn't sound like the Jo Beth I know and serve. I can't believe you're gonna let her get away with saying those lies about you to your face in public!"

"Mostly they weren't lies, Jasmine. I killed Bubba. A jury of my peers in my hometown, where I have lived my entire thirty-three years, found me guilty. It was a technicality that set me free with the help of my lawyer and Judge Dalby pulling strings. The only statement that I could find fault with was the blood-money crack, which I don't understand, but obviously she believes every word she said."

"How can you say that? You know you shot him in self-defense!"

"In a way. Listen, let's not argue. I'd much rather hear about your mother, okay?"

"There's not much to tell. My mother is a very religious person, the most religious I have ever met. I believed everything she preached and quoted from the Bible until I turned five. That was when my father went out for cigarettes and never came back.

"I loved him so much. He was a happy-go-lucky soul, and always found time to play and joke with me. I needed his laughter. My mother seldom laughed. To her, being religious meant grim warnings of perdition and

9

iron-willed determination that I would walk the straight and narrow path to redemption." Jasmine settled back on the bed.

"I really tried until my father left. I was a prim and proper religious little girl. I didn't laugh and act silly as a child. Rage and sorrow took over when I realized that he was not coming back, and that all the prayers I prayed wouldn't bring him home. Then I became a rebellious hellion, acting out and acting up. I screamed and threw fits and never flinched or cried when she tried to beat the devil out of my soul by whamming on my posterior.

"When I started school, I skipped more days than I attended. I ran away about twice a week. Once I stayed with Granny Rose for a week, and my mother didn't even bother to try and find me." Jasmine sighed.

"When I was twelve, a new preacher came to mother's church. He had a concept about disobedient children that was very close to tough love. He encouraged her to toss me out on the street and make me fend for myself. She followed his advice, had the locks changed, and refused to feed or house me even on a cold night.

"I became a prostitute to survive. I went back every once in a while, begging my mother to let me live with her again, but she never let me back in the house and has never forgiven me.

"You know the rest of the story. Hank helped me to leave the streets and co-signed a loan so I could buy my little diner. I lived there like a nun, never leaving the place except to go to church. I was afraid the city police would arrest me. With my record, they could have picked me up on the church steps. I had been a Christian

10

recluse for six years when I met you and accepted your job offer."

"My God, Jasmine. No wonder you never spoke of her, or forgave her. I would have done the same! What a terrible thing to do to your only child. She was wicked."

"You're wrong, Jo Beth. I did forgive her. I couldn't have become a Christian without forgiving her. I wanted her to forgive me, but she's never answered my letters or my knocks on her door, although I keep trying."

"You're still trying?" I couldn't believe what I was hearing.

"On the first Sunday in the month, after church."

"She's a bitch! She doesn't deserve any consideration, or an ounce of your love. Can't you understand that?"

"You're wrong, Jo Beth. She's blameless. She truly believes that I am beyond redemption. She keeps avoiding me to save her own soul and her beliefs."

"That's bull!" I yelled in anger.

"Have you ever argued religious tenets with your friends? Are you familiar with the scenario of the Chinese whore's daughter?"

"I argued religious issues long and hard in my early twenties, but not lately, and I haven't ever heard that one."

"Once upon a time in a small and remote hamlet high in the mountains of China, there lived a woman who was the village whore. The entire population treated her with dignity, as her services were needed for the single men in the village who could not find a wife. No one ever traveled to or from other cities. It was a completely isolated community.

"There wasn't a church, and Christianity was unknown. In fact, they didn't practice any type of religion. There were no radios, TVs, or communications with the outside world.

"The whore had a teenage daughter. When the daughter was old enough, the mother retired and passed on her customers to her. Question: When the daughter dies, does she go to heaven or hell?"

"Are you sure they hadn't been visited by any Jehovah's Witnesses, ringing doorbells and handing out religious pamphlets?" I quickly threw up a hand before she could respond. "Just kidding."

I pondered the enigma. "She goes to heaven. She wasn't aware that she was sinning; therefore she is without blame."

"You took the non-Christian approach. Frankly, that is the answer I lean toward, although it's not the official doctrine of the Southern Christian churches, or at least it is not the correct answer for the church I attend. They believe the girl will go to hell and burn for eternity. I think their answer is weak and you could drive a truck through their logic."

"How do they justify their belief?"

"God calls forth thousands of people each year to go forth and preach his gospel to the heathens and the uninformed. Missionaries. The Christians support and donate money for this purpose. It's tough luck for the girl that they hadn't as yet gotten to this remote village, but they're working on it. The Bible clearly states that you must be born again. That means that she has to be saved to get into heaven. Case closed."

The phone rang before I could answer. It was Sheriff Hank Cribbs.

"Hi, you busy?"

"Nope. I'm available. What's up?"

"I'd like to come by and go over something with you. Sure I won't be interrupting anything?"

"Jasmine and I were only discussing a remote Chinese village, Christian dogma, and folding unmentionables."

"Say what?"

"Being granted a visit isn't too expensive. A large deep-pan pizza with double cheese and pepperoni, please. If you still like those disgusting anchovies, remember to have them added to only one-third of the pie."

"Salad?"

"Jasmine and I will toss one here. Beer or iced tea?"

"I'm on duty. See you in thirty minutes."

Jasmine left to make the salad. I slid the drawers with the folded clothes back into place. I picked up the wastebasket, quickly picked through the items that Jasmine had tossed, and rescued about half of them. I crammed them willy-nilly into the bottom drawer.

2
"Beware of Greeks Bearing Gifts"
August 23, Friday, 12:30 P.M.

Hank arrived as I was setting the table.

"Pizza delivery!" he yelled, as he made his way through the office and stood momentarily framed in the kitchen doorway.

Hank is quite a hunk and he's well aware of this fact. As sheriff, he can wear anything he wishes but he wears the uniform of the department because he looks so good in the tailored light tan shirt and pants with a dark brown stripe down the leg. He's tall, slim and trim, with dark, flashing eyes and coal black hair.

Hank and I had an affair a while back that lasted a little longer than six weeks. We fought tooth and nail over every issue and found out that we couldn't make it as a couple. We salvaged our friendship and the only time he quits speaking to me is when he knows I've circumvented the law or lied to him. He was a rock for me during my trial and sometimes I ache for what might have been. Even as I feel regret, I know that it's ended finally and forever. He's actively seeking a wife to be the mother of the children he desires.

"You look spiffy," I said, smiling.

"Both of you are gorgeous, as you always are. I'm starved. Let's eat."

Jasmine put the salad on the table and emptied the contents of the pizza box onto our plates. I poured the iced tea and when we were seated, I asked Jasmine to say grace.

While we ate, Hank kept us entertained with a report on the latest screwup by his newest deputy.

"I told the guy to park on the corner of First Street and Highway 301, and monitor the traffic. There's been too much speeding going on. We've had two near misses out there recently, both of which could easily have produced a fatality. I told him to give it two hours and report back to me.

"Two hours or so later, he came into my office and told me that I had been correct, he had seen many speeders. He had carefully listed the cars and their speeds. I didn't believe he was serious until he handed me his notebook. His list began, 'Ford Truck sixty-five MPH in a thirty-five-MPH zone, Chevy Blazer, seventy-one MPH in a thirty-five-MPH zone,' et cetera.

"When I asked him how many summonses he had written, he looked at me askance. 'You said to monitor them. Did you want me to give them speeding tickets?'"

After the table was cleared, Jasmine left to train a class of six-month-old puppies. Hank popped into my office and returned holding a buff file folder with the usual fingerprint smudges. He must have dropped it on my desk so I wouldn't see it before eating lunch. I recognized the cover and knew it was from his department files.

I groaned audibly while slowly shaking my head.

"Hey, don't jump to conclusions. This is just to refresh my memory. I want to tell you a story."

"Sure you do."

"Don't be such a cynic. While I'm telling you about this guy, you can stop me any time and I'll go back to work and you can return to whatever you were doing before I called."

"All right." I was remembering how much time he had spent with me during my arrest when I was scared and waiting for trial. How could I stop him before he even asked for a favor? We'd been through this scenario before, but I owed him a big one, several big ones in fact.

"Whatcha got?" I made myself sound like I was interested in hearing his tale. Well, to be honest, it wasn't *all* put on; I was sorta curious. Okay, I was very curious. I reminded myself that curiosity killed the cat.

He started his presentation with a question. "Do you remember Jimmy Joe Lane?"

I gave it some thought. "I'm hearing a faint bell, but I can't bring him to mind. You'll have to tell me."

"I didn't think you'd remember him from school. He was two years ahead of you and dropped out when he was fifteen. You were thirteen when he quit, and probably still playing with dolls."

"Your memory isn't too hot either. I was playing with the likes of you and Leroy, not dolls."

Hank began humming, "Way down upon the Sewanee River."

I hit my forehead with the palm of my hand to indicate my stupidity.

"Of course, the local hero who had a ballad written about him—new words to a familiar tune—about a good man gone bad and so on. Instead of the Sewanee, it was the Okefenokee. You have to remember, Hank, when he became famous or infamous enough to have a song written about him, I had a life of my own. Not much of a life, I grant you.

"I was working two jobs, Sanders Insurance during the day and Attenburg's King Steer Steak House at night. Then came the six months' vacation lying in the hospital having surgery every couple of weeks so I could look human again after Bubba beat me up. Another six months in physical therapy before I could

16

return to work. I'm a little fuzzy on details about a bandit and a ballad during that period."

"I know," he said softly. "Did you think I had forgotten? I was right there for you, as much as I could be as a lieutenant under Sheriff Carlson."

I think I forgot to mention that Hank is also a great manipulator. I forget this character flaw when I'm recounting his virtues. I resigned myself to doing whatever he was about to ask me to do.

"Jimmy Joe Lane is thirty-five now. At eighteen, he and a former buddy got into a hassle and tried to beat each other to a pulp in the parking lot at Porky's. I had been a deputy three weeks when we got the call. Friends had waded into the fight until there were over a hundred brawling men trading punches and a lot of women pulling hair and scratching when we arrived.

"We had a first-class riot and there were only nine of us on duty. We waded in, taking our lumps like everyone else. We didn't accomplish anything but black eyes, bruises, two concussions, scraped knuckles, and a few bites from the ladies.

"Two cruisers were overturned and one was set on fire, which resulted in a total loss of one, and two out of service for several days. Sheriff Carlson was beyond anger; he was almost catatonic with hate." Hank fingered the file.

"Too many of the crowd were voters—he couldn't arrest them all—so he concentrated on the two who'd started the brawl. Jimmy Joe's opponent was a county commissioner's son, so he could only get satisfaction by focusing on Jimmy Joe. Jimmy Joe had a large faithful family behind him, but none of them had any pull. They all contributed to get him a good lawyer so he wouldn't have to use a court-appointed attorney. His lawyer bargained the charge down to simple assault, with a ninety-day sentence on the county farm. Carlson wasn't satisfied with the sentence but the district attorney hung tough, so there was nothing he could do.

"This should have been the end of it. Jimmy Joe should have served his ninety days, chalked the time up to experience, and gotten on with his life. There are some men on this earth who cannot accept confinement. Jimmy Joe was first and foremost a swamp baby, then a swamp puppy, and grew into a swamp man. He hadn't ever traveled more than sixty miles from home. He lived, ate, and breathed the swamp. He can't make it anywhere else. He walked away from the county farm after serving ten days."

"Your man sounds as if he's a couple of bricks short of having a full load. That was dumb."

"It was a dumb move, but he's far from stupid. Raised anywhere else and under different circumstances, he could have joined MENSA. His IQ is way up there. He just can't tolerate being away from his swamp."

"How long was he free?"

"Three months. He was fishing and his trolling motor quit on him. He was paddling home when the game warden happened to come his way. He was tried for escaping, and given a three-year sentence. The jails were crowded and he would have been released in about ten months, but he escaped again after serving three months. He stayed free six months and was sentenced to seven years. At this point, he owed the state ten years and two months."

"He just kept digging his grave deeper. How accurate are those IQ tests anyway?"

"His love of swamp life is stronger than his brain. He escaped from Carlton Prison after two years. He was out this time for four years and the sheriff was having duck fits about not being able to catch him. He organized midnight raids, rousted Jimmy Joe's relatives, and set up roadblocks up the ying-yang.

"This is where his followers turned him into a local hero. He sat on the bed of a friend's pickup with the tail-gate down, swinging his legs and joking with six of his buddies while they were stopped, and they were allowed to drive through four separate roadblocks. This is when the ballad was written and he became a legend." Hank took a breath.

"Jimmy Joe was now twenty-six years old, and when he was captured this time, he was given another ten years. He escaped again when he was twenty-nine, and was only free eleven days. He was still trying to work his way back home when he was recaptured. This time they gave him twenty years. He's been a good boy for six years, and this brings us up to the present. Now, at thirty-five, he owes the state more than forty years."

"This is ridiculous," I said. "The poor schmuck has served enough time for his crime. Why doesn't someone whisper into the governor's ear the circumstances of this case, and get him a pardon? Look what it's costing the state to keep him behind bars and prosecute him for his escapes. He's not violent and doesn't pose a threat to anyone. Of course, this would be using common horse sense, which no one in government seems to understand or practice. But you have a reason for telling me this story. What has he done now, escaped again?"

"Nope, it's not what he's done, it's what I think he may do. Last year, he put in a request to be moved closer to his home, citing hardship for his ailing parents to travel so far to visit. He had been held in metro Atlanta for the past six years. The request was granted at the last parole-board hearing. He was moved to Monroe Prison last Tuesday."

"Uh-oh, I see your problem."

"Yeah. The move puts him back in my bailiwick, and I don't relish the hassle and overtime I'll have, if I have to slog through the Okefenokee to find him."

"Since when have you slogged through the Oke-fenokee?"

"Well, you'd do the slogging, but I'd still have the hassle and have to pay overtime for backup. Just remember that your exorbitant fees come out of my department's budget."

Hank was referring to my contract with the county to use my bloodhounds to track down criminals, lost or otherwise.

" 'Exorbitant'? Just wait until you get my next statement for services rendered. You'll see what's exorbitant!"

"Wrong choice of word," he added hastily. "Does 'expensive' sound any better?"

"I guess. I take it that you drove out and filled me in

on Jimmy Joe's history in case he decides to escape and in case he succeeds and heads our way? Sounds a little premature to me. Maybe he's learned his lesson."

"You haven't heard the whole story, yet. I haven't told you what arrived in the mail this morning."

"Are you going to tell me . . . today?"

"Hold your horses! You're always anticipating. I want to savor this news. Seems our Jimmy Joe wrote the superintendent *weeks* ago because he wanted to add another name to the list of people who are cleared to visit him. The person he requested has been vetted and Jimmy Joe has obtained official clearance. Would you like three guesses as to whom he wishes to see?"

"Uh, the architect of the prison? A salesman for extension ladders? A friend with wire cutters? I have no idea. Enlighten me."

"You."

Hank was grinning from ear to ear. He saw that he had gotten the expression he was angling for, complete bewilderment plus a healthy dose of surprise.

"Moi?" I said dramatically, clutching my chest and widening my eyes, but it was too little, too late. My initial shock at the news delighted him. He sat there chuckling until I was ready to throttle him.

3
"A Promise to Remember"
August 23, Friday, 1:30 P.M.

You got me, I was surprised, taken aback, and completely fooled. Now may we move on?"

"If you could have seen your expression!"

"I don't know Jimmy Joe from Adam's house cat. Why do you think he wants to see me?"

"Maybe your and your bloodhounds' fame is spreading into the prisons. He might want to ask you how to keep from being captured by your hounds if he decides to break out of Monroe."

"That's a ridiculous suggestion, Hank. What could he want?"

"He might want you to start a movement to try and get him released, just like you suggested a few minutes ago, appeal to the governor or something."

"I was just supposing," I said. "I doubt if it would work anyway. That is all you can come up with?"

"I can tell you a surefire way of getting the correct answer to your question. Visiting hours are from one to four on Sunday. Go see him and find out."

"No way."

"Why not? Aren't you curious?"

"A little," I admitted, "but not enough to waste a trip out there. The place depresses me. It hasn't been that long ago that I thought I might have to live there for twenty years or so. I pass."

"You're not going to see what he wants?"

"Nope. His predicament is not any of my business. I have enough to do here without looking for more."

We were interrupted at this point when Bobby Lee and Rudy burst through their entrance door and came to meet us. Hank's face brightened, and he squatted on his heels to greet them.

"Hey, champ, how you been?" He fondled Bobby

Lee's ears. "You're wet!"

I threw Hank Bobby Lee's towel, and watched while both of them wrestled on the carpet like children.

Bobby Lee is my special love, a roommate, and a miraculous two-and-a-half-year-old bloodhound. He has over a dozen titles, and would have more if I had time to attend all the bloodhound meets. He's search and rescue trained and at this point he is at the peak of his profession, both physically and as a scent tracker. He is twenty-six inches at the shoulder, weighs one hundred and fifteen pounds, and has the wonderfully colored coat called bloodhound red.

Rudy stood by and watched the tussle of dog and man, sniffed, and strolled into the kitchen to check his food dish. He wouldn't have dampened his paws in the creek. Splashing in the dark water was abhorrent to him. He sometimes fishes off the bank at the lowest point. It's not for the food; he never eats his catch. I am inclined to guess that he loves matching his quickness with a wary trout. He scoops it up on the bank. He's never understood why Bobby Lee enjoys swimming on hot summer days. He thinks that Bobby Lee is his dog and during the first two years of Bobby Lee's blindness, he walked by his side to guide, protect, and defend.

Rudy is a twenty-pound overweight black cat with startling green eyes who appeared from out of nowhere several years ago, as feral as any bobcat in the wild. It took me months to tame him before he would let me touch him, and for him to eat and sleep inside. Bobby Lee and I let him think he's the boss and put up with his nonsense. We're family.

Hank walked to the desk and handed me the towel. Bobby Lee settled by my right side, and Rudy was back and lay curled beside me on my left.

"Want a glass of iced tea?"

"No, thank you. If you decide to go visit Jimmy Joe Lane after all, will you let me know what he wanted?"

"Of course."

"Promise?"

"Do you want me to cross my heart and hope to die if I don't? I said I would. Isn't that enough?"

Hank stood and looked uncertain. "Well, I passed on the message. I'd better be going, so you can get back to work."

"Don't hurry off. Stay awhile."

Southern manners call for a polite protest at the first mention of leaving. As I didn't press him to stay by asking him the second time, which is how you judge just how much visitors desire your company, he reluctantly departed.

Wayne and Donnie Ray were at the door before he could clear it. They stopped and greeted him.

Wayne Frazier is my kennel manager. He's twenty-two years old, bright, with a large open face, and is totally deaf. He's wonderful with the animals and I consider him indispensable. He usually has a wide infectious grin, but lately he seemed almost somber and moody. Something was bothering him and I was worried about him, but until he was ready to tell me, I couldn't pry any information out of him with a crowbar.

Donnie Ray Carver is my videographer. He is self-taught, tough and feisty, and has an ego as big as a barn.

He has blond hair and blue eyes and his mannerisms remind me of the late actor James Dean. I would have thought the girls would flock to him, but they kid him like a younger brother and try out their amateur wiles on his roommate, Wayne. Donnie and Wayne live upstairs over the garage area, to the left of the main kennel.

I made a glass of iced tea and sat at my desk waiting for them to finish their conversation with Hank.

They both flopped on the two side chairs in front of my desk looking as nervous as the cat that had just swallowed the canary.

I kept my eyes on Wayne as his hands flashed his message.

"Four out of six just qualified for their field trials, out of the C class. The trainers are running the two that failed on the one-mile search this afternoon. Nathan laid the trail yesterday."

Donnie Ray chimed in.

"The afternoon feeding is all mixed, and Doc is doing the rounds and feeding at five. He'll handle the fourth feeding for the puppies." Donnie Ray rushed his words, trying to get them all out before I could ask any questions.

I raised an eyebrow at Wayne and remained silent.

"Davis Racetrack is having a demolition derby this afternoon to make up for the rain check they passed out last Sunday."

"It starts at three," Donnie Ray added quickly.

"Then you'd better get a move on. Davis is thirty miles away. Have fun."

They both grinned and started toward the door.

"Donnie!"

He stopped in his tracks. "Yes, ma'am?"

"No speeding!"

"Yes, ma'am!"

I sat and sipped my iced tea and stared at the pile of mail centered on my desk. It was feed bills, leather-goods invoices, credit-card statements, and much more. I write checks twice a month to pay my bills. Just a few short months ago, my pulse would have raced and I would have agonized over which ones to pay, and which ones I would put off for another two weeks.

Thanks to the generosity of my late client, Ms. Can-cannon of Cat Key, I now had more than sufficient funds to operate and sustain my business. I didn't need to sweat anymore over my bank balance, but I still didn't enjoy the paperwork. I sighed and got to work. I wrote checks steadily and dutifully and tried not to mess up the computer. Wayne keeps neat, accurate records and is constantly cleaning up blunders that I commit. I am cursed with gremlins. If it has an electrical plug or operates on batteries, I'm jinxed.

I finished in time for a leisurely soak in the tub before Jasmine and Susan arrived. Friday nights are for viewing old movie classics, drinking beer, and eating pizza. The three of us are perennial losers when it comes to men. Dateless, we gather for some serious activities: gossiping, dissecting men, and pigging out.

I pulled on an old pair of white shorts that threatened to slip past my hips. I had to keep yanking the shorts up. A faded red T-shirt completed my outfit.

When Susan walked in, she eyed me critically and

gave a theatrical sigh.

"We have to go shopping, Sidden. It's becoming critical. You look as if you're dressed to paint the barn."

I gave her the once-over as I tossed pillows on the floor so we could lounge around in comfort.

Susan Comstock, my best friend since the first grade, was as fashion conscious as a New York model. She wore fabulous clothes. Her doting parents, who wished to see her married and producing grandchildren, lavishly supplemented her wardrobe.

Susan owned and managed a local bookstore, Browse and Bargain Books. Her ex-husband, Harold, ran away with a high school senior after seventeen months of marriage. Mine had lasted three years, but only because I worked like a dog to keep it going. Harold had been kind enough to stay out of the picture, but mine kept trying to beat me to a pulp. It all ended a few months back when I had finally had enough. He won't be bothering me again.

Susan was wearing a pair of mid-thigh shorts in multicolored spandex, with a matching halter top. Her brassy, carrot-colored hair was subdued with dye to a pleasant titian hue. Her bright green contacts sparkled in the muted light of the two small lamps in the office.

"You look great, as usual. In my defense, I tried to shop this morning."

I was telling her the aborted-shopping story when Jasmine arrived with a huge bowl of popcorn, butterless of course. I went to the kitchen to get drinks and to melt some butter. This time, because of my weight loss, Jasmine couldn't fuss about nutrition. In the past eight weeks, I hadn't gained an ounce, and I am keeping my fingers crossed that I don't pile the twenty or so pounds back on.

"That bitch Estelle is going to hear from me tomorrow," Susan declared. "I'm also informing her I'll never buy anything in her shop again. Ever!"

"You are a businesswoman, Susan. Stay cool, calm, and collected. You can't continue to fight my battles for me, as you did in school. Doesn't Estelle buy books from you?"

"I'll throw her out the door if she ever puts one foot in my store again. I mean it!"

"Then Estelle's cousins won't buy from you, and your cousins won't buy from her. Don't do this, Susan. You know how these feuds can escalate and last for years. Promise me you won't say a word."

"You're going to let her get away with how she treated you?"

"Oh no," I said softly. "I promise you Estelle will regret this morning. I'll take care of her in my own way and time."

"Why don't we three go to Waycross tomorrow? They have a better selection. We'll spend the day trying on dresses!"

Susan's eyes were bright from just anticipating a shopping spree. I shuddered.

"Shopping is your bag, not mine. You couldn't pay me enough to spend all day trying on clothes. I'll pop into K-mart tomorrow. If it's good enough for Jaclyn Smith, it's good enough for me."

Jasmine looked doubtful. "You don't really believe

she wears off-the-rack clothes, do you? Or, for that matter, that she actually designs the ones she hawks?"

"Maybe one or two," I said, smiling.

Susan watched her dream of shopping with us die and changed the subject.

"Did you know that Norma Jean Tramore is pregnant?"

"No," I said, shocked. I quickly counted on my fingers. "Randy has been dead six months! She didn't say a word when I ran into her while I was getting my hair cut last month. That's a shame. Randy always wanted a son. Maybe it will be a boy."

"I doubt if Randy had anything to do with it," Susan said with a winsome smile. "She's barely showing. You have to be an expert such as I to even observe the subtle changes in her waist and bustline."

"Is she dating anyone special?" I was trying to remember if I had seen her with a man in tow. I couldn't remember one.

"I have it from a good authority that she and Leon Kirkland are an item. He teaches history to tenth-graders and she is his assistant. This, of course, is not common knowledge circulating freely in their circle of friends. I understand they have been very discreet."

"How discreet is getting pregnant? Do you think that Sara knows? She and her puppy, Sherlock, are in my beginners obedience class that meets every Thursday afternoon. God!

"I wish you hadn't told me," I went on, feeling equal amounts of rage against Leon and sadness for Sara. "She told me a few weeks ago that she and Leon adored

Sherlock, that she shared my lessons with him and they were both working with Sherlock so he can pass the test next month. I won't be able to face her next Thursday!"

"Good lord, Jo Beth, you take incidents such as these so seriously. Try to be more cosmopolitan. It's not like we invented the eternal triangle here. It happens all over and usually with more frequency than you suspect. I know you're blaming Leon, but what if it's Sara's fault?"

Seeing me staring openmouthed at Susan, Jasmine intervened.

"I think Sara is nice. I've spoken to her several times. I know that you really don't know what is happening within a marriage, but she sounded so happy. I don't believe that she could have anything to do with Leon's possible defection."

"And I don't either!" I angrily agreed.

"Ladies, I apologize. I didn't mean to ruffle your feathers. I thought we were discussing the issues. See how easy it is to take sides, because you're acquainted with one or the other? I suggest we change the subject."

"Good idea."

Thirty minutes into *Dark Victory*, starring Bette Davis—a classic whose lines we almost know by heart, we've seen it so often—the phone rang.

"It's Hank," he announced quickly. "I'm damn glad to hear your voice. I'm at Dunston County High. We have a barricaded suspect with an unknown number of hostages and we're evacuating all the other rooms as we speak. Some hysterical woman kept screaming that the perp walked into the classroom with a large bloodhound and an even larger shotgun. She saw them from across the hall and ran. I thought it might be you, so that's why I'm relieved to hear your voice. I gotta go."

4
"Blood Will Flow Like Wine"
August 23, Friday, 8:30 P.M.

Hank!" I yelled loudly, to keep his attention. I knew he was trying to mentally review a dozen procedures, to make sure he was handling this right. It was sweet of him to worry that I was the one inside with the blood-hound. The phone call had wasted valuable time and he didn't need me now screaming in his ear.

"I gotta go," he repeated.

"Wait, this is pertinent! What classroom is barricaded?"

"Room 123. All it has is 'History' on the door. I don't know who is inside and what is happening. Our first priority is to clear the building."

"I know whose room it is, and who went in with the bloodhound and why. I'm on my way. Give me twenty minutes."

"Who's in there?"

"A history teacher, Leon Kirkland, his teacher's aide, Norma Jean Tramore, and Sara, Leon Kirkland's wife. She's the one with the shotgun and the bloodhound. What I don't know is, why are other people there at this time of night?"

"It's student-orientation night and their parents are supposed to come with them. School starts next week."

"That explains it. I'll be there ASAP."

"What do you think is gonna happen? Give me a clue, here."

"I think that blood is going to flow like wine. Don't storm the room. I want to try to talk to Sara." I hung up.

I turned to see two faces staring my way and two motionless bodies in the dim light.

"It seems that your gossipmonger was wrong on one point, Susan. It's obvious that Sara is now aware of what is being bandied about."

"She has the bloodhound with her?" Susan sounded as if she couldn't believe her ears.

"Of course," I said calmly. "Sherlock is family."

"I'm going with you," Jasmine stated.

"So am I!" Susan said, looking defiant.

"All right. Jasmine, get the car. I have to change. Bring my rescue suit."

Susan followed me into the bedroom. I pulled on jeans and a T-shirt.

"Why are you wearing your rescue suit? You told me that it isn't bulletproof."

"It isn't bulletproof, but it will help to slow down the pellets. I just hope the gun is loaded with bird shot and not double aught for big game."

"What's the difference?"

"Simple. Life or death. Life maybe, if you're shot with bird shot from twenty feet, death if it's double aught. It also depends on the pattern that the gun discharges, but any round at point-blank range would be deadly."

"Why are you doing this? It's not your job. Let one of

Hank's men, or Hank, do it. It's asinine to volunteer!"

"I'll try not to stand too close," I said dryly. "I know what you are thinking, that I'm doing it because I'm a hotdogger showing off. It's not true. Think it through. Hank is the most sensitive man in the entire department in regard to women's needs. But do you really believe that Sara is going to listen to any man, hand over her shotgun, and give up?"

"I don't know. What makes you think that you can do it better?"

"Because I've been there, done that, dammit! I like to think that Sara is a friend and just might listen. I hand-fed Sherlock a bottle four times a day for two weeks, when his mother didn't have enough milk for him. I want to try to get him out of that room alive."

Jasmine blew the horn at the gate and Susan and I ran for the car. The three miles to the school passed quickly. I admired Jasmine's driving. She was twenty-five years old before she learned to drive. She had asked me to teach her, and I'm so thankful that I turned her down. We had a budding friendship, and teaching a friend is dangerous to the relationship. Hank had taken over and she was a smooth, competent driver. She could even back the car quickly without weaving all over the road, which is more than I can say about some people I know.

The block surrounding the school was in chaos. Lights were pouring out every window, people were crowded on the lawn, and cars were parked and abandoned everywhere.

"Leave it here," I told Jasmine. "Just leave the keys inside and double-park. We'll have to hoof it."

We cut across the administration building's parking lot, down the south alley, and on to the back lawn, where I could see several of the local police trying to hold the impatient crowd back.

Every mother and father who didn't have a teenager in tow, or had no idea where that teenager was, was demanding to know if his or hers was being held hostage. The officers trying to keep the parents under control had no idea who was in there or what was happening.

I was saying, "Excuse me," continually to cut through the crowd. Susan and Jasmine were trying to ease by in my wake.

I had bad luck and ran into sweaty, beer-belly Floyd Graham, one of Balsa City's finest. He hates my guts. He was one of Bubba's drinking buddies, meeting behind Buford Sr.'s barn from the age of twelve. He pushed a stiff arm into my chest and stopped me on a dime.

"Hold it right there, gal. Where you think you're going?"

His body odor plus his bad breath made me fall back a step, to catch a clear lungful of air. Floyd advanced and still kept his hand on my breastbone.

"The sheriff wants to see me. Let me by."

"I see you have on your orange playsuit that you sport around in, but what I don't see is any of your mangy hounds. Gonna use your own nose this time?"

"Let me pass, you poor excuse for a human being, or so help me God, Floyd, I'll plant your balls in your rectum. Get out of my way!"

Susan suddenly appeared right in his face and let go with a bloodcurdling scream. It startled Floyd so, he stumbled backward, almost losing his balance. It was so unexpected that I stood riveted in place. Both Susan and Jasmine grabbed my arms and began to propel me across the lawn. Soon the three of us were running freely for the back steps of the school.

"Warn me next time," I told Susan, panting, when we arrived at the door. "I still can't hear in my left ear!"

"Just remember, surprise works just as well as threats!" She cackled with glee. "I could get into this very easily. See what you've been missing by not taking me along?"

"Oh God," I said to Jasmine. "I've created a monster. Give me some help here."

"Susan, you were marvelous!" Jasmine enthused.

"You call that help?"

"Here comes Hank," Susan said.

He frowned as he approached us. "What are you doing in your rescue suit? You don't possibly think I'm going to let you walk into that room, do you? Why did you bring Jasmine and Susan? I've got enough to worry about in trying to figure out who in my department is informing GIB of my every move. Fray is on the way."

John Fray is in charge of the Waycross field office of the GBI, Georgia Bureau of Investigation. We call them GIB, and the FBI, the Federal Bureau of Investigation, FIB, to show our contempt.

"Where is he now?" Agent Fray is a horse's ass and causes me a great deal of distress when he pokes his nose into our local problems.

"About ten minutes out of Waycross, burning up the pavement to get here. He's bringing a quote, negotiator, unquote. I'm not to do anything until he arrives."

"We have a good forty minutes. Which room are they in?" I asked, peering down the hall. Lieutenant J. C. Sirmans, Hank's second-in-command, was leaning against the wall about fifteen feet away, at the next juncture, a hall leading to the left. I started his way.

"Jo Beth," Hank whispered urgently. "Come back. I don't want you walking in there. Maybe we *should* wait for the negotiator."

I walked back and stood toe to toe with him and put my hands on my hips.

"How many do you think will die in there if we wait too long, or get Sara more agitated than she already is? I'll talk to her outside the door. Let's see what she has to say. I will seem less threatening than a stranger."

He laid a hand on my shoulder. "I knew I wouldn't win this argument from the get go. If you're going to talk to her, I'm going to know what is going on."

He motioned to J.C. and he began to tiptoe toward us.

"J.C. has a wire. J.C., I want to be able to hear what she's saying."

"Hurry up, J.C.," I said impatiently, "the meter is running." He picked up the kit, and began taping the mike to my T-shirt, and dropped the battery pack in an inside pocket of my jumpsuit. In less than five minutes, he announced that he could hear me fine. He had the equipment spread out on a desk in the first room to the right.

"Just to the door, Sidden," Hank said gruffly.

"Gotcha," I replied, crossing my fingers in front of me

as I walked slowly up the hall.

When I reached room 123, I placed my ear against the door and strained to hear through the thick oak. This building was built in the 1940s, and had been renovated from time to time, but all the doors, casings, and window frames were the original oak, which seemed impervious to time.

I knocked softly three times and listened. I could hear nothing. I turned the knob slowly and found the door was not locked. I glanced back to see if Hank was watching me, but he must have been in the schoolroom listening with J.C.

I put my lips to the crack between the door and the frame.

"Sara, it's Jo Beth, your dog trainer. Can I come in and talk?"

I placed my ear at the crack and heard nothing. I waited a few seconds and repeated my message.

I glanced at my watch. Ten of my forty minutes were gone. What could they be doing in there? I agonized again over how many parents and children were inside with Sara, her bloodhound, her bridegroom, and his paramour.

I was undecided. Should I or shouldn't I? I wasn't getting anywhere standing outside the door. Surely Sara wouldn't shoot me if I eased inside. No, I couldn't count on Sara. She also wouldn't walk into her husband's classroom with a shotgun, but it seemed she had, so guessing what she would do was out the window.

I had to make a decision. Fray would be here soon and he would take over, and Hank and I would be shunted to the sidelines to stand and helplessly watch whatever unfolded.

There were faint noises coming from the street. Car motors running, an occasional horn, and some low murmurs from the restless crowd.

The almost silence began to gnaw at me. The halls, during school hours usually teeming with children's voices and locker doors slamming, started feeling spooky. I found myself holding my breath so I could listen more intently.

I braced myself, took a deep breath, and pulled the doorknob and eased the cracked door open. I entered and silently closed the door before I turned around and looked into the room. The adrenaline was flooding my circulatory system nicely and I sucked in another deep breath before trusting my voice.

"Hello, Sara."

5

"Would She or Wouldn't She?"
August 23, Friday, 9:20 P.M.

The three major participants in this tragedy were up front, by Leon's desk. Leon and Norma Jean were sitting with their legs crossed, their knees against the wall and their backs to the room. The blackboard was above them. They both turned their heads my way, and they looked scared to death. Their hands were folded in their laps and they sat like statues. After recognizing me, they swiveled their heads back in front of them and stared at the wall.

Sara was turned, facing the door, looking at me and slouching in Leon's chair, the shotgun resting across her legs with her finger inside the trigger guard. Her face was pale, but otherwise she looked calm and exactly like she did when she tilted her head a little to listen to my advice in the north field where I held my training class.

I took a quick glance to the left to see how many were in the room. They were clumped together in the right rear of the room, each in a seat with their arms folded. I counted a total of twelve. They were sitting very still but I could hear that some of them were sniffling, whimpering, and softly sobbing. I didn't have time to see if I knew them or whether they were parents or students. I turned my gaze on Sara.

She smiled at me. "What are you doing here, Jo Beth? Have I got one of your relatives sitting back there?"

"No." My voice was giving me trouble, and I coughed to cover my nervousness. "I came to help you." I glanced down at Sherlock, who was curled in sleep. His lead was fastened to her chair.

"Why did you bring Sherlock?"

"I almost didn't, but now I'm glad I did. If this family is breaking up, he should be on hand to see it, shouldn't he?"

"He won't understand, Sara. He'll be scared if you shoot that gun. He hasn't had any training under fire. We don't need him here, so why don't you let me call Jasmine? She's just down the hall and can take him for a walk." I forced a smile. "He probably has to pee by now."

She laughed easily. "Is that why you're here, to rescue Sherlock? You shouldn't have bothered. He's my dog now, and he goes where I say."

"God, Sara," I said sadly, "don't be so selfish. I fed him a bottle by hand four times a day for over two weeks. Don't you think I want him to live? You have twelve hostages sitting in the right rear of this classroom, your husband and his teaching assistant up front, sitting on the floor and facing the wall. No one knows why you're doing this."

I gave the head count and their positions for Hank, who hopefully was hearing every word.

"I came here tonight to celebrate the end of my honeymoon. It's supposed to last a year, but mine didn't quite make it, did it, darling?"

I swear her voice sounded normal, just like casual conversation among friends. I felt chill bumps lightly scamper up my arms. This lady I didn't know. I had no idea what this one was capable of. She was too quiet and composed.

Leon turned his head to his left and licked his lips.

"Sara, honey, you have to believe me. I'm not having an affair. I swear to you, I don't care what Myra told you, it's not true. Please, please listen. I love you."

"Leon, dear, if you turn your head and speak one more time, I will make you eat this shotgun barrel. Didn't I make this perfectly clear?"

Leon had sounded sincere to me, but I guess if I were in his shoes, I'd be striving for an Oscar performance also.

Leon turned, facing the wall, and I heard muted sobbing. I wondered if he was telling the truth and all the accusations were false. That would be a fine kettle of fish. I stole a glance at Norma Jean Tramore, who was sitting on the floor, to his right. Her eyes were closed and she looked frozen with shock. She wouldn't be any help in this and I just prayed that she would remain as still as she was and not freak out.

"So," I said, casually, "this is about something that someone named Myra told you? Is this Myra reliable? I don't know about you, but I believed Leon, myself. He seems to love you very much."

Now I could only pray that both of them would deny everything until we could get the shotgun out of her hands.

"Jo Beth, don't tell me that you haven't heard about Leon and Norma Jean and also about the baby."

Something changed in her voice when she said the word "baby." My heart beat a little faster and I sensed that this meeting was not going to end well.

Since Sara hadn't moved the shotgun that rested across her legs, I glanced back at the hostages. I saw two men who could pose an immediate problem. They were gripping the small desks and eyeing each other.

I decided I better get the message to them loud and clear.

"No one in this room should move an inch," I stressed, "until this dispute has been resolved. No, Sara, in answer to your question, I haven't heard a word of gossip about you or your husband, Leon. What's this about a baby? Surely you can't believe this nonsense! Norma Jean's husband has been dead less than six months. Who is this Myra, anyway?"

"She's my best friend, Jo Beth. Myra Steelman? You know her and her husband, Norman. She said everyone in town knew but me and that she couldn't keep it a secret any longer, that I had to be told."

"Then why isn't she here by your side, helping you correct the matter?"

I bit my lip. I sounded too confrontational. The last thing I wanted to do was to get her moving toward a quick solution.

"I didn't tell her what I was going to do. It didn't cross my mind to invite her to come with me."

It may have been my imagination but she sounded just a tiny bit hesitant. I had to jump in with both feet.

"Well, deep down, I bet you don't feel she's your best friend, or you would have," I asserted. I didn't know where this was going; I was winging it. I had passed the hostage-negotiation seminar rooms when I was walking down the hallways of the GBI academy on the way to the dog-handler seminar rooms. I was now wishing I had sat in on a couple or three.

"Let's let the hostages decide," I offered suddenly. "You wanted an audience to hear your accusations or you would have let them leave. How about it, do you want me to poll them for their answers? Let's see who they believe, your husband or your best friend. I bet they haven't heard any rumors about you and Leon either!"

I couldn't have made it any clearer. I didn't want anyone to admit that they had heard anything. Sara, still slouched, swung her chair around and seemed to notice them for the first time.

"No," she said softly, "I don't think so."

"Why not? They've heard everything that has been said in here."

"I don't want to hear them speak. I may have to shoot them later."

"Shoot them?" I choked out.

"Lady, I need—"

One of the two I was worried about had half-risen out of his chair and begun talking. Sara had pivoted in her chair and clasped the gun to her chest. I stared at her trigger finger with morbid fascination. He shut up when she started moving and eased back into his seat. I was a good twelve feet away and still saw the sweat pop out on his forehead. She finally lowered the gun back into her lap.

"Can I let Jasmine take Sherlock for a walk? She'll bring him right back."

Sara looked at her dog. "Wanna go out?"

I hoped that if I could get her to release someone, I would have a chance to get some others out. I started with Sherlock because I thought he would be the easiest.

Sherlock popped up like toast and started what I call the wiggle dance, twisting his body in anticipation. I was hovering over him, releasing his leash from the chair, before I realized I had moved. I rubbed his silken ears.

"I'll just walk him to the door."

It was hard to turn my back on her. At the doorway, I opened it only wide enough for Sherlock to pass through and handed the lead to the right. It was grabbed forcibly from my fingers and I saw Hank in a blur, reaching for my wrist. I jerked backward and quickly slammed the door and turned the lock.

When I turned to face Sara, I saw her smile.

"You love Sherlock, don't you?"

She sounded so normal that my heart soared.

"You bet." I grinned back at her. "Now let's do this right. As of now, I'm your best friend through thick or thin. We're gonna get rid of the bunch of onlookers in the back. Sara, these people are not interested in your dilemma. They're frightened and want to go home and eat supper. We just need the four of us here to get to the bottom of these rumors that your so-called friend Myra told you."

She seemed to be listening, but hadn't indicated whether my plan met with her approval or whether she might start pulling the trigger.

"Everyone stand up slowly and form a line, children first. Don't speak and don't run."

I raised my arms like I was gathering a choir to its feet. The group rose dutifully and a boy about sixteen started forward. One of the men I had had my eye on previously reached out and drew the kid to his side. They both started forward.

I wished to God that I knew the position of Sara's shotgun at that moment. I was afraid to look at her; it might make her do something foolish. Believe me, if I'd had a gun at that moment I would have been tempted to pull the trigger myself, on either an over-protective papa or a craven man who wanted out of here as quickly as possible—take your pick.

I felt I had to gain control quickly.

"Step to the end of the line, mister. I said children first."

"I'm going with him," he blustered.

We all heard a deadly sound. It beats all to hell and back the sound of a rattler singing in your ear. It was the quick ratchet of the shotgun as Sara primed the pump.

My heart stopped and I turned to face her. With twelve feet between us, she could cut down half of us with the first discharge. It didn't matter if it was bird shot or double-aught buckshot. The pattern wouldn't have time to spread in so short a distance.

"Do what Jo Beth said," Sara stated calmly. The gun was up to her right shoulder. "Move to the rear of the line."

The man stumbled backward, trying to put other bodies in her line of fire. I saw two more kids coming forward and beginning to form a line. I walked to the first boy and started the slow march to the door. I didn't look back.

Unlocking and cracking the door a few inches, I stood directly behind it and used my right hand to locate a shoulder and guide it through the small opening. I concentrated on counting as they disappeared from my vision. I knew hands were pulling them to safety but I didn't know whose.

I had hold of the seventh shoulder when I heard an irate whisper in my right ear.

"You saved the damn hound before you did us!"

I turned and looked into the drawn features of Estelle

45

Cully, who just this morning had booted me out of her boutique. *Just this morning? It now seemed eons ago.*

"Hurry up before I change my mind," I said through gritted teeth as I put my hand in the small of her back and pushed. I received satisfaction from her surprised yelp as she was almost pulled off her feet by unseen hands.

When the twelfth person was out and I was bringing my arm inside to secure the lock, the door was bumped and I flung out a hand to steady myself. I was grabbed and went sailing out in the hall like I was on greased skids. I sprawled on my hands and knees before more hands pulled me erect and started hustling me around the corner.

"Let me go. I can get them out of there. Turn me loose!"

I was struggling with whoever was holding me. Since I could see Hank in front of me, I appealed to him.

"Let me go back. Please, Hank. I can talk her out, I know I can."

"You're lucky you didn't get anyone killed. I should be arresting you for obstruction. If you don't shut up and behave, that is exactly what will happen."

Agent Fray of GIB was holding me in an iron grip. I looked back at him and glared.

"Take your hands off me *now,* you son of a bitch!"

Both arms were released. I saw that Lieutenant J.C. Sirmans was the other culprit. He gave me an apologetic shrug. "Sorry."

I ignored both of them, and again appealed to Hank.

"Please, Hank?"

"Can't do it, Jo Beth. It's Fray's case now. She still has two hostages in there. Thanks for getting all the others out. They owe you their lives, every one of them."

"I don't even know who half of them were," I replied plaintively. "I wasn't watching their faces. I just wanted them all out."

I turned to Fray. "You better pray that all three walk out of there, because if even one gets hurt, I'll make you pay, Fray. That's a promise."

"That's a lot of crap," he said. "You don't know if you could've—"

The blast seemed to roll down the hall, gathering momentum in its path and blowing past us. Hank's eyes met mine in consternation, and we stood, breathless, staring at each other in shock. The second explosion seemed muted because our ears were still ringing and deadened from the first. We hadn't moved when the final sound we were dreading pounded against our senses.

6
"Looking for Someone to Blame"
August 24, Saturday, 8:30 A.M.

Balsa City mourned the death of three of its citizens. The paper had banner headlines and lots of editorials and sidebars about their senseless deaths. Fred Stoker, the editor of the *Dunston County Daily Times*, must have worked all night. One story speculated that Sara was of unsound mind when she killed her husband, his assistant, and herself.

That wasn't such a hot bit of news. Everyone who kills has to be temporarily out of his or her mind to commit such an act. Fred was treading lightly over the grimmer aspects, such as why she blew them and herself away. He has a philosophy of protecting the surviving family members from unnecessary grief.

I called. I knew that even if he hadn't had a wink of sleep all night, he would still be manning the phone. The paper and its readers are his life.

"Hi, Fred, it's Jo Beth. You didn't get much sleep last night, did you?"

"Twenty years ago I wouldn't have blinked over losing a whole night's sleep. At sixty-six, it will take me three days to recover. I plan to nap by the phone all day. I would have called you earlier, but I was afraid that you might be sleeping late this morning."

"Fred, I'm mad at that pig from GIB. I guess you've heard the story by now."

"I heard it last night almost as it was happening. Aggie was on the cell phone and I was typing her copy directly into Bessie."

"Bessie?"

"Had a milk cow named Bessie that I had to milk twice a day, back when I was a callow youth. She was ornery, prone to having sensitive teats, and tried to kick my backside over the stall on many occasions. My computer reminds me of her, hence the name."

"I'm surprised that you admit to having difficulties operating one. I thought I was the only klutz in town."

"Jo Beth, everyone who has ever fingered a computer

keyboard has had difficulty with them. The ones who won't admit it are lying. It's like the new owner of a sports car who goes back to the dealer complaining that he isn't getting the fabulous savings on his gas mileage that other owners are achieving. The dealer tells him to do like the successful owners do. When he asks what, the dealer says, 'Lie.'"

"Yeah, sounds about right," I replied. "What are we gonna do about Fray? He is the biggest screwup I've had the misfortune to meet. We're gonna have to do something that will get him transferred."

"Unfortunately, we don't have a Siberia that we could have him exiled to. We both love this area, but Waycross is about the end of the line. You can't send him to a smaller station, or a less significant one. He's here already."

"Then we'll have to get him fired. He has to go."

"I think that he would be hard to con. He has no imagination. A man who doesn't dream doesn't fall easily for a bag of tricks."

"Give me an example."

"Well, I wasn't thinking on it, but the old standby comes to mind."

"Which is?" I prompted.

"We find out when Fray is going to spend a night in one of our motels. We take our town drunk, Fred, get him tanked and drive him by the hospital so a nurse can shave every hair from his body, then drop him in Fray's bed, naked as a jaybird.

"We'd have to slip a Mickey in Fray's coffee—I understand he doesn't drink—and tuck Fred in bed with

49

Fray. Leave two empty scotch bottles, apply lipstick on the appropriate areas, and remove all clothing from the room.

"Then we hand Aggie her camera and a tip that a wanted felon is in the room. She can convince two of Balsa City's finest to break in without a search warrant. Voilà! Agent Fray doesn't work here anymore."

"God, Fred, I had no idea you were so devious; it's perfect! My only objection would be treating our resident drunk, Fred, that way. I like him."

"So do I. Fred would volunteer for the duty if you explained. Fray ran into him last summer and got him thirty days in the city lockup, where the average temperature in the cells is a hundred and ten degrees at three P.M. I try to watch over Fred. He's my namesake."

"He's named after you?"

"Yep. Fred's mother was so happy that I wrote a story about her winning the Bible in Sunday school *and* spelled her name correctly, she named her firstborn son Fred. He looks much older but must be around thirty-seven now."

"What was his mother's name?"

"Calladittywah."

"I'll take your word for it. What happened after Jasmine, Susan, and J.C. wrestled me out of there last night?"

"I was told Fray was very unhappy with you kicking him on his shins. Seems you got him twice, before the others got you away from him. He was threatening to have you arrested for a while, but Hank finally got him calmed down. Hank had to write up the reports, and

Fray just copied the highlights into his. I hope I'm still around when Hank gets enough of him."

"Fray will never get to Hank, he's too professional. Had you heard the rumors about Leon and Norma Jean and that she was pregnant?"

"Between Aggie and me, we know everything that goes on in this town. I had an interesting phone call this morning from someone who *hadn't* heard the rumor until last night. It was Norma Jean's younger sister, May Ann. Do you know her?"

"Yes, she married a guy from Mercer."

"May Ann was almost hysterical with grief, and when she heard the rumor about her sister being pregnant, she said she had to tell everyone that it was a lie. Poor thing, she wanted me to run a story in the newspaper that said it wasn't true. I had to tell her I couldn't do it, and she was ready to spit in my eye."

"How could she be so sure that Norma Jean wasn't pregnant?"

"Because last Thursday Norma Jean called her and asked her if she could come over and take care of her because she was having a bad day with the vapors."

"Vapors?" I didn't believe what I was hearing.

"Jo Beth, I'm mod. I'm hip. I'm cool. I'm also a Southern gentleman who still finds it awkward discussing ladies' bodily functions with a woman half my age."

"Menstrual cramps?"

"Correct. May Ann put her to bed, produced pillows, made hot cups of tea, kept the hot-water bottles full of hot water, and made her as comfortable as possible. She said she hated to leave her, but that Norma Jean sent her home in time for her to cook her husband's supper."

"So Norma Jean wasn't pregnant," I repeated dully.

"That's my assumption."

"If she wasn't pregnant, maybe she wasn't having an affair with Leon. Wouldn't that be a hoot?"

"May Ann assured me that in their frequent talks, Norma Jean really seemed to like Leon a lot but that it was more of a brother-sister thing, not sex or the pull of passion."

"So, someone invented a vicious rumor that spread like wildfire and caused three people's death?"

"Possibly . . . indirectly," Fred said softly.

"To hell with indirectly," I said, trembling with emotion, "I only see cause and effect. It was murder."

"I'm afraid you're incorrect. Stretching it, it might be called depraved indifference, but no one would ever suffer jail time because they started a rumor."

"You may be wrong on that assumption," I said grimly. "Rumors have to start somewhere. All you would have to do is trace it back to someone who can't name a source."

"It would all be for naught, my dear. You cannot bring the dead back or punish the perpetrator."

"You're probably right, Fred. Listen, I enjoyed our conversation very much. It's been too long. I'll call you again soon."

"Jo Beth . . ."

"Yes?"

"Take care."

"You too."

I called Hank. His phone was finally answered by a deputy who informed me that Hank was out with Agent Fray and not expected back for at least two hours. I wondered what motel Fray used when he stayed in Balsa City to keep from driving sixty miles home late and sixty miles back early.

I called Susan.

"You busy?" Susan was usually alone at the bookshop in the mornings.

"Nope. Wasn't last night terrible? Jasmine and I heard the blast way out on the lawn. When we got inside, you were the only person I could focus on. It must have been that Day-Glo orange suit. We both thought that you might have been inside when the shots were fired. I have heard from several people this morning what a heroine you are! The paper didn't give you enough praise."

"Lord knows, I didn't want praise, just to get everyone out alive, and I didn't even accomplish that. I got some shocking news this morning."

"What?"

"Norma Jean wasn't pregnant, and if she wasn't pregnant, she might not have been having an affair with Leon. How about them apples?"

"Who said she wasn't pregnant?"

"A very reliable source, I've been told." I was going to start being more discreet in the future and not blab every rumor or conjecture that I heard.

"I'm sure my source is more reliable than your source," she said complacently.

"Come on," I said jokingly, "who told you?"

"I won't be spreading rumors for a while, I'm afraid. My source will remain unnamed, just like yours. I feel bad that I had told you and Jasmine less than an hour before the shooting started."

"You know I won't spread it around, Susan. Give!"

"You have no intention of telling me where you got your information, why should I tell you mine?"

"Because I know when to keep my trap shut!" I retorted angrily. I bit my lip.

"I knew you were interrogating me, I just knew it!" she exclaimed in triumph. "You're gonna track down whoever started this rumor, aren't you? Your sense of right and wrong is stronger than that of the rest of us mortals. The sainted avenger strikes again!"

"You're dead wrong. Don't take that attitude, I was simply being curious. Also, you goaded me into saying what I did about my trap, admit it!"

"Yeah," she said, trying to sound forgiving, "I did, so you're off the hook for the mean remark."

Tell me another one, I thought wearily. I'd be apologizing for what I said for the next year. Now I thought I'd try to spread more salve on the wound.

"I have a great plan for getting rid of Fray, the horse's ass. Would you like to conspire with me to bring him down?"

God, what was I doing? I now had both feet in my mouth. Susan was one of the last people I would turn to for help in any conspiracy.

"I'd have to think about it. Tell me the plan." She seemed to be interested.

"Gotcha," I cried. "Just kidding! Wanna have lunch?"

The line was silent. Susan had hung up on me.

7
"A Visit with Jimmy Joe"
August 25, Sunday, 2:30 P.M.

I had told myself that I wasn't about to go see what Jimmy Joe Lane wanted to talk about and truly believed it up until two P.M. At that point, I gave a fatalistic shrug, took a shower, and was now tooling along at fifty on a two-lane blacktop that led to Monroe Prison.

Taking my time, it would be a forty-minute drive. The temperature was in the high eighties but the wind was blowing from the northeast and I was comfortable without using the air. Low humidity made a bad tracking day, but coupled with a breeze it made the heat bearable.

I was driving my car because when locals spotted the van and had the time, they sometimes followed it because of the sheriff's department seal and the black outline of a bloodhound painted on each side. Today it would have been mostly teenagers or singles in their early twenties, bored with small-town Sunday afternoon somnolence and craving excitement.

By the time I had checked in, been patted down for drugs by a female guard, and shown into the waiting hall, it was three fifteen. The crowd was thinning. Visiting hours were from one to four. I sat at a picnic table and listened for my name.

A tinny muted voice saying "Joel Simon" floated on the air and over my head. Only when they repeated it and the small green light winked on over the fifth booth did I realize they meant me. I rose and walked to the metal straight chair and stared at the stranger sitting behind a thick glass partition, his features screwed into a large feckless grin.

He was overdoing his welcome. He reminded me of my mother's admonishment when I was six and was manipulating my face to show my anger at a playmate. "Goodness, child, what if it suddenly grew cold and your face froze in that position? Wouldn't that be a sight?"

I didn't remember Jimmy Joe from school. To the best of my knowledge, I had never laid eyes on him. His dark hair was shorn so close to his scalp that half the area seemed bald. His eyebrows were too thick and lush to match his denuded head. A sallow complexion was proof that he hadn't been exposed to the hot Georgia sun for ages. I thought back to the timetable from Hank's briefing. It had been six years, if I remembered correctly, since Jimmy Joe had been out, which only counted for eleven days of freedom and then three more years.

His faded jumpsuit was not the faint gray of the other prisoners; it was the same garish Day-Glo orange of my rescue suit. This meant he was prone to run, and they wanted to be damned sure that he could be easily seen while doing so.

I guessed—as best I could given that he was sitting—that he was my height and weighed about 140 pounds.

I pulled out the heavy chair, sat down, and raised an inquiring eyebrow. He quickly picked up the phone on his side of the glass, put it to his ear, and gestured toward the one by my right hand. I picked it up and spoke first.

"Are you Jimmy Joe Lane?"

"Yes'm, and I'm real proud to meet you at last. I surely admire your skills with dogs and I've kept a scrapbook of all your exploits that appeared in the *Atlanta-Constitution* and the *Dunston County Daily Times*."

"I admire kind words, as most folks do, but I'm sure they weren't the reason that you asked to see me. What's on your mind?"

"I wanted to be sure that you knew I admired you so if you get upset with what I'm gonna tell you, you won't leave without knowing how I feel about you."

"All right."

I sat and waited for him to get to the point. He placed both elbows on the narrow ledge in front of the glass and tilted his head to the receiver and gave me another huge grin.

"Do you remember reading about me? Nothing much for the last six years, but I've been cussed and discussed a few times myself. Do you remember the song they wrote about me?"

"I didn't remember you at all. Sheriff Cribbs had to fill me in. Now, what is it that you wanted to tell me that might make me angry? This is not a social visit."

"I'm messing this up and I apologize. The only women I've talked to in the last seventeen years were kin to me, with the exception of a few female guards. I'm nervous. I'll just blurt it out and hope you don't get down on me.

I wanted to tell you I'll be leaving here soon, and I love dogs. I had bluetick hounds when I was growing up. I have never mistreated a dog in my life, honest. Don't put any of your dogs on my trail . . . please?"

I stared at him. I couldn't believe he could be so dumb and here Hank had been telling me how brainy he was. I shook my head in disbelief.

"You are nuts! First, you tell a complete stranger you're planning on trying to escape from here, and second, you have the unmitigated gall to threaten my bloodhounds!"

"You're not a stranger to me, ma'am; I've loved you for six years. You're on my mind every waking minute of my day. I surely don't want to harm them bloodhounds of yours and that's gospel. You surely wouldn't feel kindly toward my proposal of marriage if I did, I'm sure of that! I didn't want to tell you so soon about awanting to marry you and all, but you sounded so riled I had to let you know that my intentions were honorable."

I stood quickly, shoving the metal chair, which made a penetrating screech, like chalk drawn across a blackboard. My legs had worked faster than my brain in assembling his crazy message. I still had the speakerphone in my hand.

"I don't know you and have no desire to hear another word out of your mouth. I will report your conversation to the warden about a possible attempt to escape. If you should succeed in breaking out, my bloodhounds will track you in or out of the Okefenokee and run you to ground. That's not a threat, it's a promise!"

I slammed the phone harder than necessary in its cradle, spun on my heel, and didn't stop until I reached the information counter near the front entrance. This gave me time to control my breathing and calm down.

Two women in front of me were chattering in Spanish and gesturing at their wristwatches. They seemed to be angry. I glanced at my watch and saw that it was ten minutes until four. My guess was that the guards had refused to send for whomever they wanted to see and they were protesting that it was still visiting hours for another ten minutes.

A bored guard slowly picked up the phone and requested an interpreter. He waved them aside and looked in my direction. I cocked my head to indicate the far end of the counter and walked several feet from the women and waited for him to follow me. He eventually moseyed on down to me, shaking his head.

"They don't understand English, lady, so why did we have to move down here?"

"I doubt that. How many foreign women have you met in their early twenties that don't understand English well enough to get by? I just didn't want what I had to tell you to be overheard and repeated to any prisoners."

"Why would they pretend not to understand me?"

He was not only bored but also pissed that he had been asked to walk a few extra feet and then had to lean over the counter to hear me.

"They were late getting here and are still counting on being able to see their men. They're using their minority status to get special privileges."

"Never happen," he asserted. "Now, what's this earth-shattering piece of news that you didn't want spread to the prison population?"

I changed my mind. This guy was an idiot.

"I would like to speak to the warden," I said, pronouncing each word distinctly.

A loud raucous buzzer sounded for a good five seconds, making me nearly jump out of my skin.

"End of visiting hours," he explained, sneering because the racket had made me twitchy. "The warden doesn't come in on Sundays."

"Okay," I said, being reasonable. "Make it the assistant warden."

"He doesn't work on Sunday afternoons."

"Captain of the guard?" I hazarded.

"On vacation this week."

Answer Man was having fun. He cocked his head and waited for my next guess. I should have dressed better. I wasn't being taken seriously in worn jeans, T-shirt, and cross trainers in nightmare orange.

"To whom would I report a future jail break?" I asked politely.

"Me," he answered, not batting an eyelash.

"You?" I repeated skeptically.

"Uh-huh."

"Perhaps you should get pen and paper, so you won't forget," I suggested sweetly.

"I'll remember."

"A recent transferee from Atlanta, Jimmy Joe Lane, was telling me he's gonna walk soon. He also mentioned my bloodhounds, in passing. I have the contract for search and rescue for this prison. My name is Jo Beth Sidden."

"Uh-huh."

"That's it? 'Uh-huh?' "

"Uh-huh."

We both turned toward the loud conversation that began when a prison guard approached the waiting women. All three were speaking at the same time, and all energetically waving their arms. Answer Man and I couldn't understand the words, but knowing the general drift of their request, it was easy to follow their progress by watching expressions and hand movements. With less than sixty seconds of rapid-fire negotiations, all three were smiling happily as the guard led them away toward the visitors' area.

"Mission accomplished," I remarked.

His look of consternation changed to aggravation.

"Anything else?"

"I want to apologize. I didn't take into consideration that you might not be able to read or write. Shall I write the message and leave it with you?"

His seventeen-inch collar seemed to shrink. Suddenly a dull flush began to creep upward from his neck to his hairline. I've found that younger men will shrug off an insult better than older men will; the young hate to let the female know she has scored. This one was pushing fifty.

He gripped the counter until his knuckles were white and didn't trust himself to speak. I decided to get out of there. It isn't wise to insult a prison guard while you're locked inside his place of employment.

I was halfway home before I began to see the humor

in the situation. Jimmy Joe was a cocky little bastard. I began to chuckle at his positive attitude toward escape and his building of air castles about a future romance with yours truly. I decided right then and there that if he ever succeeded in making his way back to his beloved swamp, I just might not be the one to bring him back. I forgave him for warning me not to use my bloodhounds. I didn't doubt his love of hounds for a minute.

I was feeling quite mellow when I arrived home. If I had known what was in store for me, I would have been wailing and gnashing my teeth. But, as they say around here when something is unexplainable, "Who knows what evil lurks in the hearts of men? The Shadow knows."

8
"A Broken Promise"
August 25, Sunday, 7:00 P.M.

Jasmine and I decided to eat out, so we went to Pete's Deli for babyback ribs, corn on the cob, coleslaw, and beer. I had the beer; Jasmine drank iced tea.

We had chosen a booth on the right and I was sitting facing the doorway. When I saw Brian Colby enter, my gut began to clench even before I spotted Susan directly behind him.

"Susan just arrived with sleazebag Brian. Prepare to smile and make nice."

"Lord, you were right. Behave . . ." Jasmine murmured.

A while back, Brian had been a bone of contention

that almost ruined my friendship with Susan forever. My intuition—based on Colby's possessive attitude toward Susan—made me suspect that Colby preyed on women. I had Hank check him out, and he confirmed my suspicions—Brian had a history of cozying up to women, and then bilking them of their money. Hank had run him out of town and Susan was furious that I had interfered. Now he was back. I'd have to grin and bear it.

"Hey, if it isn't the dog lady! Howdy, Jo Beth!"

"How are you?" I said as I shook his outstretched hand. I gave a startled Susan a warm smile and held it in place as I stared into Brian's eyes.

"Oh, I just keep turning up like a bad penny." He gave an affable chuckle as he placed his arm around Susan. "I bet you never expected to see me again!" He not only wanted to pour salt on the wound, he wanted to rub it in.

"I was sure you'd be back"—I leaned toward him as if I was delivering confidential information—"Susan's too valuable."

His eyes narrowed to conceal his hatred. He got my message, Jasmine got my message; in fact, all of God's children got my message except Susan. Her face was flushed with pleasure that Brian and I had obviously buried the hatchet. Little did she know that we both wished we could bury it between each other's shoulder blades.

"Join us?"

"Thanks, but not tonight." Brian answered without consulting Susan. "We have so much catching up to do, but you be sure to call us, you hear?"

He turned Susan adroitly, heading for the rear dining room where the tables had candles and were barely large enough for two.

"Take a deep breath," Jasmine suggested, "you're turning blue."

"Did you hear that cocky bastard? 'Call us.' I'd like to ring his worthless neck!"

"Do you think she's let him move in with her?"

"No way. Her parents are not only old-fashioned—they are positively Victorian. To them, their image is everything. They want her married and having grand-children, not shacking up with a jerk who can't commit. Thank God they still have control over the purse strings. They pay her credit card bills and receive copies of every charge. Brian could only take her for a few hundred before Daddy would tumble to it and go after him with tar and feathers as he had him ridden out of town on a rail."

"He could still stay over on the sly."

"Did I mention that Mommy hand-selects and pays for Susan's daily maid, who cleans, does laundry, picks up dry cleaning, shops to stock refrigerator and larder, and probably listens to Susan's voice mail?"

"I wouldn't think that Susan would put up with so many restrictions in her life."

I smiled. "Unlimited charge accounts for clothes, trips to New York, cuddled and cared about? It's mildly annoying, but she's their only chick and she loves them. She explains that she's spending her inheritance as she goes."

"I gather they wouldn't approve of Brian?"

"I honestly don't know. I do believe that her daddy would tie the money up where he couldn't gut her estate and would also demand a prenuptial agreement. That would upset Brian, but he's forty and may want to come in out of the cold. Pickings must be getting slim for him to return to a town where the sheriff knows his record and has run him off once. I love Susan, but she's a lousy judge of men."

Jasmine grabbed her napkin and covered her mouth.

"Jesus, just listen to me! The pot calling the kettle black. I'm a fine one to judge, aren't I?"

Jasmine drank some water and smiled weakly. She still didn't trust her voice.

"You want dessert? Let's take home ice cream. Fudge ripple okay?"

I grabbed the check and paid at the desk with my Visa card. Then I had to stand patiently while Jasmine counted out her half of the check into my hand. She never lets me get away with treating except on her birthday.

I was turning left off Bloodhound Lane onto the paved courtyard when I heard Jasmine gasp. It was a little after eight and just dark enough for the night lights to be a hindrance instead of a help. I had my gaze on the chain-link fence post so I wouldn't turn too quickly.

I looked up as the headlights swept the area where everyone parks when they arrive. We had company. Sheriff Hank Cribbs's official car and two other vehicles, which had the state seal in bright letters, were parked and three men in uniforms stood together eyeing our approach. They weren't smiling.

"Oops," I whispered.

"You didn't wear your pager?" Jasmine sounded shocked. "Hank looks angry."

I'm subjected to being called out for search and rescue twenty-four hours a day, seven days a week. I have a contract for three counties.

"I forgot it, okay? The worst they can do is shoot me. You take the ice cream in and put it in the freezer, then come back out. We may both have to go."

I slid out of the seat and approached the men. Jasmine had understated Hank's expression. He wasn't angry; he was furious. The taller of the two others wore a captain's bars, and when I was near enough to read their patches, I saw they were from Monroe, where I had visited Jimmy Joe. I guessed they were here to check out the message I'd left for the captain of the guard.

The captain spoke before I could greet them.

"Are you Jo Beth Sidden?"

"Yes, I am," I returned pleasantly. "Are you here to check on the message I left at the information desk this afternoon?"

"What message?" he snapped.

"If you aren't here about the report I left, then why are you here?" I delivered my question as briskly as he had spoken and managed to sound almost as snotty.

He reached into his tunic pocket and placed a folded piece of paper into my hand as he spoke.

"I have a search warrant signed by Judge Perry to search your property."

"Why?" was all I could manage. Bewildered, I glanced at Hank and he stared back without any apparent change in his expression. Suddenly I knew. I felt laughter bubbling unbidden in my throat and fought the giggles.

"He escaped?" I consulted my watch. "Four and a half hours after he informed me of his intentions, he's gone? In broad daylight?"

I couldn't hold back the tide any longer. My laughter filled the warm humid air. I literally laughed until I cried. Digging a tissue out of my jeans, I dried my blurred eyes and it finally dawned on me that I was the only one making a noise. I listened to the ominous silence. Peering at my solemn audience, I moved a languid wrist.

"You really had to be there," I began lamely, and then totally lost it, again.

I felt my feet momentarily leave the ground and my shoulder being pressed against the car window. The skyline tilted. The captain had thrown me against Hank's unit and was in the process of handcuffing my wrists.

I heard a swoosh of air released from his lungs and saw him stagger sideways as Hank knocked aside his handcuffs and grabbed a handful of his shirt.

"What the hell do you think you're doing?" Hank inquired angrily. He pointed his left index finger silently at the other guard when it appeared he was going to join in the altercation. The guard quickly changed his mind when he saw Hank's pointing finger and stood rooted to the asphalt. Hank glared at the captain.

"You don't lay a hand on a citizen in my county who hasn't broken a law. You gonna arrest her for laughing?

Let me know what citation you'll be quoting for cuffing her and I'll look it up. None comes to mind."

"Let go of my shirt," the captain demanded.

"Only after you apologize to the lady."

He thought about it. "Sorry," he muttered briefly. Hank let loose of the shirt and the captain began to nervously press the wrinkled fabric with both hands.

"She was impeding a state investigation for an escaped felon and possibly aiding and abetting," he said, trying it on for size.

"Bullshit!" Hank declared. "You had served her with a legal search warrant. You don't need her permission. Search away. But remember two rules. One, don't open any drawers or cabinets and riffle through any clothing, if the space being searched is not large enough to hold a one-hundred-and-forty-pound male. Second, you don't disturb the items on top of dressers, tables, desktops, and kitchen cabinets, or rake same onto the floor where they could be 'accidentally' stepped on. Are we clear on these points?"

"Maybe I should shove a broom up my ass and sweep the floor while I search," the captain snarled in disgust. "Jesus H. Christ, whose side are you on anyway?"

"Law and order, Cap, and I follow the rules."

The captain conferred briefly with his buddy and they split, the captain heading toward the house and the other moving to the kennel.

I wanted to bat my eyelashes and whisper "My hero" to josh Hank into a better mood, but a glance at his thunderous expression changed my mind. I decided to sound properly penitent as I apologized.

"I'm sorry, Hank, I was planning on telling you tonight when we got home. I didn't decide to go to the prison until the last minute this afternoon. . . ."

My explanation trailed off when I saw his contempt.

"What?"

"You promised me you would let me know when you visited. You didn't. I was just wondering why I still believe that you're gonna tell me what really happens and keep me informed. I should know better!"

He held up a hand to stem the flow of my excuses. "Just answer my questions. Are you gonna search for Jimmy Joe Lane, if asked?"

"No."

"Will they find him on your property?"

"No."

"Did you help in any way in his escape or give him information he would need to leave the prison property?"

"Et tu, Brutus?" I was getting pissed.

"That doesn't answer my question."

"No, no, no. Is that clear enough?"

"Monroe could cancel your contract if you refuse to search."

"Screw 'em. I've had three call-outs from Monroe in the past two years. They're not exactly furnishing Kibbles 'n Bits for my kennel."

"All the contractors could cancel."

"Screw 'em all, including the Dunston County Sheriff's Department, and the horse you rode in on! It must be really tiresome to be the perfect-sheriff-who-makes-no-mistakes Cribbs. I'm tired of apologizing

69

every time I see your mug. In fact, I'm tired of seeing your face. When you finish with this current chore, do me a favor and stay the hell away from me!"

I turned and started toward the back door and almost ran into Jasmine on the way back out from putting away the ice cream.

I gave her questioning look a "Later," and stepped up on the back porch where my two roommates, Bobbie Lee and Rudy, were patiently waiting for my return.

"I'm gonna have some ice cream, you want some?"

They both beat me to the refrigerator.

9
"Second Guessing"
August 25, Sunday, 8:30 P.M.

I removed the half gallon of ice cream from the freezer, dug out a scoop each for Bobby Lee and Rudy and three for myself. I sat at the kitchen table and watched them bolt down their share and then move to their regular spots, Rudy on my left and Bobby Lee on my right. Tonight they sat closer than usual and leaned lovingly against my leg.

"You're both adorable, but you don't get any of mine."

I sat in the kitchen staring off into space for over an hour and brooded. Finally bored, I moved into my office. Rudy had given up the vigil long ago and had left to nap on my bed. Bobby Lee was dozing, leaning on my knee for support and emitting an occasional snore. Bloodhounds can sleep anywhere, even standing on their feet, if they can just lean against something. He followed me and stretched out on my right.

The captain of the guard had spent less than ten minutes searching the house. There are only a few places that a man could hide in my house. Hank had taken all the fun away by warning the captain that he wouldn't be able to trash the rooms, leaving them looking like a hurricane had blown everything on the floor and smashed half of the breakables. Thank God, the search warrant had stated that the premises could only be searched for a fugitive. If it had permitted a complete search for any signs or clues that he had been here, it would have taken all of us at least three days to put everything back and clean up.

I shouldn't have let Hank get to me. It was just that I had gotten so angry when he cut off my explanation about why I hadn't told him of my prison visit. I had planned to call him at home when Jasmine and I returned from supper. I did have over an hour at home this afternoon, but instead of calling him, I had soaked in a warm bubble bath and inhaled three cold beers before leaving for Pete's. That's what Sundays were for.

I had been waiting to tell Jasmine the full story tonight, when I knew she would crack up over my smitten suitor and his premature proposal. Now she was out there watching them search and didn't know a blessed thing about what was going down.

I should have been out there with them, but she had Hank, Wayne, and Donnie Ray with her. I would be a liability. If I saw either one of the uniforms knee or shove a dog, I would have to spend the night in jail for battery on a law-enforcement officer.

It was after eleven when I heard car doors slamming and engines being started. I went to the back of the office and peeked out through the window blinds. The prison vehicles were backing and turning and going out the driveway. Hank was standing by his unit talking to Jasmine. I didn't see Wayne or Donnie Ray, so they must have gone upstairs to their apartment. Hank finished talking and gave Jasmine a tight hug. They were both laughing when he slid behind the wheel and left. Jasmine stood there until he was out of sight. I hurried back to my desk and propped my feet up and tried to look relaxed when she entered.

"They have any luck?"

"If you mean did they find Jimmy Joe Lane, the escaped prisoner, did you really expect them to? There could have been twenty adult elephants a few feet back in the brush of old-growth forest inside your fence and they wouldn't have known.

"Hank was kind enough to point out this fact to them, when they halfheartedly shined their flashlights on the edge of the clearing and didn't set a foot inside the uncleared area. The captain mumbled that they would be back with twenty men to search the area at daybreak, but Hank doesn't expect them to return." She grinned.

"Hank told me to tell you that in case Jimmy Joe *was* back there, you should warn him so he could clear out before daylight."

"Very funny," I said wryly. "Did dear ol' Hank have any more words of wisdom for me?"

"He said that he was pissed at you and you were pissed at him but that was SOP, so I shouldn't fret."

"Ready for some fudge ripple?"

"No, I need coffee, tons of coffee, and not the debugged kind. I need caffeine. I'm still shaking."

"It's warm out," I stated, filling the coffeemaker in the office.

"My shakes are from nerves, not goose bumps. I want to drink coffee and hear every word about what happened today, and especially about the 'message' you tried to tell the males about before they cut you off at the knees."

I looked up from the coffeepot in surprise.

"I can't believe my ears. Are you really saying that Hank did something wrong?"

"He be a man, don't he?" she said solemnly.

I laughed. "Bless you. I think it's the first time you've ever taken my side when Hank and I were fighting."

I handed her the cup of delicious-smelling coffee, and fixed one for myself. I might not sleep for hours, but this was an occasion. I recounted Jimmy Joe's odyssey and the entire visit at the prison. She shook her head at Jimmy Joe's forty-odd years left to serve for simple assault and his audacity in disappearing right under the guards' noses.

"Do you really think he was successful in escaping, or is he hiding somewhere on the grounds and hoping he can get out after the excitement dies down?"

"He's had six years to plan this. He has a large, close-knit family that is willing to help him. I don't know how he pulled it off, but I believe he's celebrating freedom right now in the Okefenokee Swamp with a few close relatives and friends." I lifted my coffee cup. "Here's to Jimmy Joe. May he live a long and happy life free of restraints!"

"Hear, hear!" Jasmine agreed. "Were you serious about not going after him, if the powers that be should ask?"

"Absolutely. I really didn't appreciate the search warrant. I can only guess what happened with the message I left at the information desk. Either the guard ignored it, or he left a message on the captain's desk and when Jimmy Joe was discovered missing, the captain checked the visitors' log and decided that I helped him somehow."

Jasmine frowned. "They found him missing very quickly. Did he trip an alarm or something?"

"They have an early meal for supper on Sunday afternoon, right after visiting hours end. They have the lockdown count at five P.M. I suppose that is when they found him missing. God, he really had to be touched in the head to try to escape in broad daylight when he knew they would discover his absence within the hour. So far he seems to be successful. Course Hank wouldn't call to tell me if they already had him in custody. I imagine the only news we'll get will be from the newspaper and the radio station."

"After hearing what was going on, I understand now what the captain meant by 'What message?' He really did seem surprised."

"I agree with you. I don't think he knew anything about my message, but then again, he may have but thought I was trying to throw him off the scent. Who knows?"

Jasmine smiled. "Tell me what you think of your newest admirer."

"Don't you dare tease me about his confession of undying love for me. Tell me why I'm so unlucky in the men who seem to be attracted to me. Is it something I say or do?"

"I'm not going near that question, thank you very much." Jasmine yawned and stretched like a cat. "I'm exhausted, and have an eight A.M. class. I'm gonna hit the sack. Need anything before I go?"

"Not a thing. I'll see you tomorrow. Sleep tight."

She trudged off to bed and Bobby Lee and Rudy left for their late-night run. I didn't wait up for their return. I undressed, crawled under the sheet, and prepared to spend a long time before I slept. I went out like a light. I awoke once during the night from the nightmare that visited at least once a week.

Bubba was moving toward me in slow motion, his bat poised to clobber Jasmine. I pushed her away lightly and she floated out of my vision as I slowly fired six rounds into his torso. Bubba clutched me in his fatal fall and the copious flow of his blood covered me like a soggy blanket.

I awoke in a cold sweat and trembling from fear. I exchanged yellow-colored sheets for white ones with blue sprigs of summer flowers and pink shorty pajamas for light green. I lay back down to rest, knowing sleep would be impossible. I drifted off near dawn.

10
"Saying Good-bye"
August 26, Monday, 8:00 A.M.

I slept in this morning. After the late night *and* an unwelcome nightmare, I felt quite peaked. After three cups of coffee and a bowl of cornflakes with a banana, I began to feel somewhat human again.

I read the paper with my coffee. If I hadn't been informed last evening about the "Great Escape" I could have easily missed the short two-paragraph report on page three. Fred's front and second pages were devoted to the tragedy of three of our townspeople shot and killed in a high-school history room. The funeral announcements were heavily outlined in black, with pictures directly above each notice. The ghouls would be disappointed with the coverage. Fred had avoided any mention of how or where they died, nothing about a shotgun or gore, and had affixed no blame. This was for the local families who could clip the articles and have them Xeroxed and encased in plastic for the family albums.

I dreaded funerals and today I had three to attend. Leon Kirkland's parents refused to let Sara be buried next to Leon and also wouldn't let her be a part of his service. Sara would be buried in her parents' plot and her funeral would be at eleven A.M. Leon's funeral was at one P.M., and Norma Jean Tramore, a widow of six months, would be buried beside her husband, Randy. Who would have thought that they would both die in the same year?

The phone rang before I finished the paper. A female

voice asked for Jo Beth Sidden.

"This is she speaking."

She asked me to hold for Warden Sikes, Monroe Prison. Aha! Jimmy Joe had been found within the wire and I was gonna get an apology, or he was still missing and the warden wanted me to find him. Either way, it was payback time. I'd met Sikes during past searches. He seemed to be a nice, polite person and had admired the bloodhounds.

"Ms. Sidden, Warden Sikes. How are you?"

"I'm fine, sir."

"I want to apologize for the misunderstanding last night. Captain Jenkins just transferred here this spring and he wasn't aware that you did our searches for missing prisoners. He was, ah, a trifle hasty securing the search warrant, without my permission. The incident would not have happened had I been here."

"I accept your explanation, sir."

"Has Sheriff Cribbs notified you that we are now ready for you to search for this prisoner?"

"No, sir."

"We have scoured the grounds with no success. It's obvious that he has freed himself and we have no idea how he did it. How many men do you need to go with you and when can we expect you?"

"I won't be available for a search for Jimmy Joe Lane."

"Did I hear you correctly? Did you say you wouldn't search for him?"

"That's correct."

His tone of voice was sharper and he sounded surprised.

"May I ask why?"

"For several reasons. Just be assured that I won't be able to help you."

"It is my understanding that you signed a contract that still has three or more years to run. Is this correct?"

"Perfectly correct."

I was going to make him work for every answer that I gave him and volunteer no additional information. His voice was now cool and had a crisp snap.

"Will you explain your failure to fulfill this request for assistance?"

"No, sir."

"What?"

"No, sir, I will not explain."

"This is ridiculous. I'll get back to you shortly!"

I listened to silence and smiled. I gently replaced the receiver.

When I entered the grooming room, Wayne informed me that Sara Kirkland's parents had picked up Sherlock earlier.

"Did they say why," I quickly signed, "or leave a message?"

"Mrs. Watson said she was taking him to the funeral." Mrs. Watson was Sara's mother.

I groaned. "Did she mention if she was going to bring him back?" Wayne gave a negative shake of his head and looked questioningly at me to fill him in.

"Beats me. Maybe I'll get a chance to ask her today," I said.

I wanted to know what was in Sherlock's future. I would be glad to buy him back.

The relatives of Sara and Leon were feuding with each other instead of dealing with their grief. I was going to try to track down the vicious rumor that had destroyed their children's lives. I just hoped that they wouldn't fight over Sherlock. Sara's parents were too old to work and train him; they were both in their early sixties. Sherlock had progressed well with his basic obedience training. He was alert and willing and would make an excellent search dog.

I hated to think of what he would be like in a year if they decided to make him the family pet as a monument to Sara's memory. He would be overweight, wouldn't have enough exercise, and would have lost his edge to learn and be trained even if they finally agreed to try. I made a mental note to myself to go visit them in a couple of weeks and try to explain what he needed.

After a brief inspection of the kennel, I was walking back across the courtyard when a blue car nosed around the corner from the drive. It slowly pulled up to where I was heading to the back-porch sidewalk.

I went around to the front of the car while a man unfolded long legs and stood up beside the opened door. He was very tall. I had to keep adjusting my vision upward until he finally finished straightening to his full height.

He was over six feet; I would guess by five to six inches. He had broad shoulders and looked like a college basketball player twenty years down the road who had maintained his waistline but had lost the battle to keep his hair. His hairline had receded. What hair was left was dark and he had unusual light green eyes and was a total stranger. I stared at the eyes a tad too long. He gave me a small smile.

"Everyone assumes they're contacts, but they are inherited from a northern Celt and a Scottish lass, or maybe it's the other way around. I'm not sure."

"They're beautiful," I blurted, feeling the color creep up my neck. "I'm Jo Beth Sidden. How can I help you?"

"I'm Leland Kirkland, Leon's oldest brother. Please call me Lee."

"I'm called Jo Beth. I'm so sorry for your loss."

"Thank you. You never expect your baby brother to die first. I understand you tried to get everyone out. I want to thank you for the ones you saved."

"I hoped to save all of them, but a slug who's an agent for the GBI yanked me out prematurely and I didn't get a chance to try."

"You did good. Mom saved the paper for me."

"You're not local, then? You're just here for the funeral?"

Why don't you ask the guy a few questions? I thought with irony. Jesus.

"I live in Fox Grove. Know it?" I shook my head no. "It's almost three hundred miles to the north, in the mountains. I visit Mom and Dad two or three times a year, now that they are getting older. Leon's death just moved my scheduled visit up a few weeks."

"Leon was a couple of grades ahead of me in school and you said you're the oldest brother. If you went to school here, I was probably running around barefoot and with pigtails."

"I'm sorry that I don't remember you, just as you

don't remember me. Right?"

I smiled. "Right."

"Mom and Dad sent me on an errand. They want me to pick up Leon's dog, Sherlock, and pay the kennel fees for boarding him."

Uh-oh. I must have looked surprised.

"He is here, isn't he?"

"Not exactly."

"No?" It was his turn to look surprised.

"Sara's mother and father picked him up over an hour ago. My kennel manager, Wayne Frazier, told me that they wanted him at the funeral."

"You're kidding!"

"I'm afraid not."

Lee focused on the tarmac and moved a foot back and forth absentmindedly.

"Is the dog valuable?"

"If you mean money-wise, I really don't think that's the reason both sets of parents want possession. They are all hurting right now, blaming each other and trying to assuage their pain with anger."

"I'm just trying to understand what's going on. Legally, who gets the dog?"

"That's going to be touchy, if they're gonna fight for possession. I'm not sure, but I would think that *if* Sara and Leon had a reciprocal agreement that everything goes to the other, Sara survived Leon—but since she was the cause of his death, she doesn't stand to gain from her crime." I gave him a straight look.

"I'm really worried about Sherlock. He's a very talented dog, and with another month of hard work, he

81

should finish his obedience trials. If he's going to be in limbo for months while the court settles a civil dispute, he might not ever achieve his potential."

"Couldn't you board him here and keep up his training until they decide who inherits?"

I smiled. "It's not that simple. It takes a great deal of time, commitment, stamina, and money."

"How much time?"

I laughed. "I think I know what you're thinking. I really couldn't explain a bloodhound's needs in less than two or three hours and we both have funerals to attend today. Why don't we have lunch later this week? How long are you planning on staying?"

"My first game is in three weeks, but I should get back before then. I'm a high school football coach. I will be staying for a few days. I'll call you about lunch."

"Great." I glanced at my watch. "I'm sorry that I don't have time to visit with you longer. I have to get dressed for Sara's funeral. Will I see you there?"

"My mom would disown me. Personally, I liked Sara, but under the circumstances I couldn't go."

"I understand."

He left and I stood there gazing after him. I'd asked almost everything but the most important question, did he have a wife? I had left this too late to work it in smoothly without being obvious.

Why would I even be thinking along those lines anyway? I'd had a long-distance romance with Jonathan that had withered on the vine because of a lengthy commute; it would be foolish to even contemplate another. I should forget that Lee was the first to even stir any interest, lo these many months, and those wonderful green eyes, the broad shoulders, et cetera, et cetera. I went to take a cold shower.

11
"Comforting the Survivors"
August 26, Monday, 12:20 P.M.

Susan and I had sat together in the fifth row of All Souls, and were now strolling among large pine trees to the graveyard, two hundred yards behind the church, where Sara would be laid to rest. Bright sunlight and high humidity. We were both eyeing the black smudges that were moving in slowly from the east.

"What's our chance of getting damp?" Susan asked idly.

"Thirty percent this afternoon, and fifty tonight."

"You obviously disagree, since I see your umbrella in your bag."

"Just prudent. They're guessing along with the rest of us. I've been in toad stranglers when they predicted thirty."

"You're getting older and more cautious, Sidden. An umbrella *and* flat heels? Where's your adventurous spirit?"

"I'm not risking a sprained ankle from stepping into an armadillo hole out here. We have two more cemeteries to walk through this afternoon. You can live dangerously if you wish. I knew you were gonna mention my choice of footwear before the day was over," I grumbled, "and slow down, I'm beginning to sweat!"

She laughed and we slowed our pace until we reached the large open-sided green tent. Millers' Brothers Mortuary had arranged about fifty folding chairs inside and a good two hundred had attended the service. We stood with the overflow in the sunshine and listened to Reverend Williams's brief summation of Sara's life.

When the long line began forming to walk by the immediate family, seated directly in front of the casket, I halted Susan and turned her back toward the church.

"We'll have to pass on offering our final condolences. That line will take an hour. Everyone says a few words, and some say more than a few. Mrs. Watson also has Sherlock sitting in front of her knees. He seems to be behaving, but I'd hate to make him break training if I walked up close to him. He knows my smell and he might be bored. We have twenty minutes to reach Gospel Holiness downtown or we'll be late and I don't want to be late."

Susan hesitated. "I wouldn't mind missing Leon's service. I'm still angry with him over the way he treated Sara."

"The way he was *rumored* to have been treating Sara. Anyway, if you don't go, you will possibly miss meeting the man I might marry sometime in the future."

I had taken several steps into the trees before she could catch up with me and halt my progress.

"YOU MIGHT MARRY . . . WHO?"

"Lower your voice," I said, laughing. "It's too soon to be announcing my coming nuptials. For all I know, he may be already married. I just met him this morning."

Susan dramatically placed a hand over her heart and groaned.

"One of these days!" she threatened. "First thought that entered my mind was that you meant the idiot who just escaped from prison, your long-term admirer from afar. Is he still loose?"

"I guess so. I haven't been told differently."

"You really aren't going to help them look for him?"

"Nope. I didn't appreciate their attitude."

"I talked briefly to Hank last night. He mentioned that *your* attitude left a lot to be desired—but I'm with you, to hell with them!"

"Thanks," I said dryly. "Now if you'd just change *your* attitude and tell me who told you about the love triangle . . ."

We had reached her car. She unlocked it, slipped in quickly, turned her key, and started the engine. We stood with the doors open and the air conditioner on high to dispel the pent-up humid August heat. When the air was bearable to breathe, we climbed in just as a single large drop of rain splattered against the windshield.

Susan had ignored my last question while maneuvering her Lumina minivan out of the church parking lot. I decided not to push her for an answer. She'd tell me in time.

I once again admired the pristine condition of her car. She had it washed once a week, detailed and simonized monthly, and was a fanatic about maintenance. It looked just as good today as when she'd driven it out of the dealership.

"How many miles have you racked up on this thing?"

Her gaze dropped automatically to the odometer before she answered, but I bet she already knew within fifty miles.

"Eighteen thousand plus. She's been mine for three months now."

"You've had this one for over three years!"

"After thirty-six payments to the bank, Miriam and I are debt free."

"Don't you want a new model?"

"I hate car payments. Miriam and I are going to grow old together. Don't ever mention trading in her presence again."

I laughed. Wayne and Donnie kept all our vehicles running smoothly, but they had dents, scratches, the odd burns from my smoking days, and a great many more miles on their meters.

"You never told me about the guy you met this morning," she reminded me. She changed the wipers from intermediate to high, as the water was now sluicing down the glass, softening the lovebugs that were stuck to the pane's surface from the ride so far today and that would haunt us for the next three weeks. We were in the middle of our second lovebug attack of the year. She changed the air vents to blow on the windshield because the quick change from hot air to cool water was making the glass fog.

"His name is Leland Kirkland. He's Leon's elder brother, who's home for the funeral. He lives in the extreme north portion of the state. If I can ascertain that he's not married, engaged, living with someone, or seriously committed, I am going to have lunch with him this week."

"Jesus, why bother? You've already gone the long-distance dating commute with Jonathan. Are you a glutton for punishment?"

"You haven't seen him," I said smugly.

"So he's a hunk, so what? Why don't you do your shopping locally?"

"Susan, you're my best friend, and I want you to remain my best friend," I explained wearily. "I have to be honest here. I don't think the pot can call the kettle black, if you get my drift. I'm not Julia Roberts in looks and temperament, and Brian Colby is not Hugh Grant. Let's practice a little tolerance."

After a deafening silence, she finally answered in a faint voice.

"Touché."

We were lucky in finding an empty parking place almost beside the canopied sidewalk. Susan reached under her seat and groped around for her umbrella and muttered with disgust when her hand came up empty. I pushed on my door, opened it, and ran around to her side. We huddled close under my umbrella's cover until we reached shelter.

The temperature had plummeted ten degrees in fifteen minutes. The wind had picked up and was blowing spray the width of the walkway. We hurried close to the inner edge and were both wet from our hips to our toes by the time we entered the church vestibule.

I stacked my wet umbrella against the wall with the others and brushed ineffectively at my damp, navy voile skirt. Maybe it wouldn't shrink too much above my

87

knees. I caught a glimpse of my hair in the hall mirror and felt despair. The heavy moisture had turned my smooth hairdo into a riotous mass of kinky curls.

"I know what you're thinking, Sidden, and it isn't that bad," Susan whispered.

"The hell it isn't," I hissed softly, momentarily forgetting my hallowed surroundings.

We were seated near the front, only four pews back from the immediate family. We were on time, but most of the attendees were still on their way, driving slowly because of the heavy deluge of water.

Out of the blue I remembered a cute story I had read years ago of a millionaire's funeral in a cold northern state, in January. He had asked to be buried on the coldest day of the month, when the worst weather conditions prevailed. Only three had attended the outdoor interment in the family burial vault: a nurse, an elderly housekeeper, and his limousine driver. They were very startled later when they were informed that they were to share equally in his twenty-million-dollar fortune.

I smiled as I remembered. That couldn't happen in a small Southern town in Georgia. We take funerals of townsfolk as a sacred commitment. We go to see and be seen. No telling what you would miss if you skipped one because of a little rain and wind. We have attended during hurricane warnings, tornado watches, and all other disasters, mainly because the surviving family members would never forgive you if you stayed home.

Susan leaned close and mouthed into my ear, "Point him out."

"He's to the left of his mother."

"He's bald!" she said, sounding surprised.

"No, he isn't," I said with a smile. "He has a high forehead."

She rolled her eyes upward at my nonsense. I glanced back. The church was slowly but surely filling. It would be another twenty minutes or so before the services could be started. I wondered if I had time to dash to the bathroom. I discussed it with Susan and we both decided to go. She asked the lady sitting next to her to save our seats.

The rest rooms were off a corridor on the right, and when we entered, the four stalls were full and several women were at the long dressing table trying to repair the wind and rain damage to their makeup and hairdos.

I recognized one of Leon's first cousins and flinched when I saw her turn her angry countenance on Susan.

"Well, I hope you're satisfied, Susan. Spreading all those lies about Leon got him killed! Florence told me what you said about him. You should be ashamed of yourself!"

Susan stood frozen in shock. You could have heard a pin drop on the indoor-outdoor carpet. A few seconds later she regained her poise.

"And you are . . . ." she replied unemotionally.

"Oh, you wouldn't know her, Susan," I drawled. "Edna doesn't read, so she wouldn't frequent a bookstore. Maybe we should all take up a collection and buy her a Ms. Manners book on etiquette, if they print one with lots of illustrations."

"You stay out of this, Jo Beth! You're not the hotshot you think you are. You saved the hostages and even the damn dog. Why couldn't you have saved Leon?"

A woman standing next to her and having a strong family resemblance put a hand on Edna's shoulder, which she angrily shrugged off.

"You owe Susan an apology, Edna," I said quietly. "If I were you, I think I'd ask Florence who-all she told, and then check who they told. I wouldn't be surprised to find out that you confided in a few more yourself. Come along, Susan, we don't want to be late in paying our respects. Ladies."

When Susan and I were back in our seats, I reached for her hand and squeezed it gently.

She managed a wan smile. "Thanks."

"Forget it. Consider the source."

During the service, I happened to glance her way and saw tears brimming her eyelids. I wanted to throttle Edna for being such a bitch. Half the town had contributed to the tragedy. I vowed silently that I would never again ask her who had told her and would stop trying to find out how the vicious rumor had started. A lot of people were suffering and any action on my part couldn't bring back the three people who had died.

Reverend Willis announced that the graveside services had been canceled due to the inclement weather. We began lining up to speak to the family, and say our farewells to Leon.

I had always believed, even as a child, that viewing the body in the casket was a barbaric ritual. Prettying up a corpse, dressing it in pastels or backless business suits, and displaying it on padded satin seems a bit much. Some of our townspeople still practiced the old ways of bringing the body home and sitting up all night with relatives and friends. To each his own, but I had made it quite plain in my burial instructions that my casket would be sealed.

I looked ahead and noted that Edna was not in the receiving line. Since Leon's parents, two brothers, and a sister were there, no cousins were needed to represent the family. I was relieved. I wouldn't put it past Edna to make a public scene as Susan was passing. I focused on the flowers that were at each end of Leon's casket. I had no desire to view his remains. Instead, I remembered the sunny afternoon just five months ago that he came with Sara to pick up Sherlock from the kennel.

He had laughed and held Sherlock and was surprised by the loose wrinkled-skin soft bundle of fur. That's the way I'd remember him.

We moved past the family, briefly touching hands and patting shoulders, and I nodded with sympathy when we reached Leland. Both Susan I and took a deep breath of the rain-laden air when we reached the sidewalk. Two funerals down and one to go. A truly depressing day.

12
"A Puzzling Incident"
August 27, Tuesday, 8:15 A.M.

I was up with the birds, but it was after eight when I sent Bobby Lee to fetch his lead. When I joined him on the back porch, he seemed puzzled. He looked at me and back to the post where both leads usually hung, as if asking what was going on. Both nails were empty.

91

"Where are your leads?"

He whined once and stood on his hind legs as if he was confirming that they were not there.

"Let's go see Wayne. Maybe he's cleaning them or something."

Donnie Ray was steaming the dirty bowls from breakfast and Wayne was weighing a litter of three-month-old pups. Some kept wiggling out of the cart and others were trying to climb back in. We watched until he had finished.

"Good morning," I said aloud and signed to Wayne. "Do you have Bobby Lee's leads?"

He pointed to a grooming table with a frown and began signing.

"They were in the middle of the floor in here this morning when I came in at seven."

I glanced at Bobby Lee and back at Wayne.

He wasn't smiling. "They were neatly coiled, and not damp with saliva."

I knew that Bobby Lee was incapable of neatly coiling the leads. Even if he had accomplished that feat, it would have had to have happened the night before if they were dry. Just taking them off the nails he got them wet.

"What's your guess?"

I couldn't think of anything. I was coming up empty.

Wayne shrugged and looked worried.

"Maybe Bobby Lee is asking for a raise," Donnie joked.

"He's too proud of being able to fetch them off the nail. He couldn't and wouldn't do something like this."

Wayne signed his agreement.

I glanced around, trying to make sense of what had occurred.

"Everything else is in place?" They both nodded.

"Jasmine left early for a drug search at United Chemical. She didn't have any ideas, either."

"Are all the trainers here this morning?"

"Everyone but W.A."

W. A. Beekham always ran late. He took care of his father, who was confined to a wheelchair. I understood his problem and let him make up the time when he could. I shook my head.

"A mystery. Maybe we'll find out something later. I'm gonna train the six-month class."

I had finished with my charges and was back in the house cleaning up when Jasmine arrived around half-past ten. We discussed the misplaced leads.

"It doesn't make sense," Jasmine said when she found I was clueless.

"Agreed. I can't think of any explanation."

I turned in my chair and stared out at the warm sunshine. All the clouds had passed and it was becoming another sultry August day.

"You know, lately I feel as if I'm exuding some kooky kind of essence around here. I don't know, it seems that I'm drawing weirdos into my orbit."

Jasmine looked a little uncertain. "Are you turning fey on me?"

"What have I done, that I rate that mentally deficient Jimmy Joe claiming his undying affection and trying to entrap me in some sort of conspiracy?"

"Have you heard anything more on his escape?"

"Nobody tells me anything," I said moodily.

"Hank hasn't called?"

"Nope."

"Why don't you call him?"

I sighed. "I've been dreading it, but I guess I'll have to if I'm gonna find out what's going on."

I dialed his number.

"Cribbs."

"Are you still speaking to me?" I tried to sound contrite.

"Of course," he answered evenly. "How can I help you?"

"I'm sorry I took out my frustration about the search warrant on you. Will you forgive me?"

"Certainly."

Uh-oh. He was still mad.

"Have you heard anything more about our escapee?"

"I guess he's still missing. I haven't heard differently. Their silence is unusual. I thought they would be screaming for your head on a platter. They haven't even officially requested my office to mount a search."

"The warden called me and requested one."

"What did you tell him?"

"No soap."

"How did he take it?"

"He threatened to cancel the contract and hung up."

"I heard that he called the county commissioner's office and complained that you refused a call out."

"I bet your snitch was your third cousin, once removed, from your mother's side. She still works in the office?"

"She's not a snitch, she's family." He sounded complacent.

I was envious of his close-knit extended family.

"If I had your connections, I would own the county by now," I said dryly.

"Nah, you'd be worn out trying to run everyone's life."

"You think?" I countered.

Hank laughed. "If I hear anything, I'll let you know."

"Thanks."

I hung up and glanced at Jasmine. "He hasn't heard a peep."

"Strange. It's almost like they're ashamed of losing him so quickly, so they're laying low and keeping mum. I'm going to make a fresh pot of coffee."

"Good idea."

I was idly turning over the pile of mail from this morning, stacking the bills and throwing out the advertising fliers and other junk mail. Halfway down the pile was a regular-size plain white envelope with my name and address printed in pencil. There was no return address or postmark.

I was curious and reached for the letter opener. Pulling out a single, ruled sheet of notepaper, I scanned the few lines and closed my eyes.

I must have made a noise of some kind, because I felt Jasmine's hand on my shoulder and the paper being removed from my fingers. I looked up at her as she read the contents aloud.

Missy,
Y'all are a sound-sleeping bunch. Your dogs are

*too friendly for their own good, especially the one
that lives in your house. He brought me his lead and
gave me the grand tour. He's a mighty fine dog.
Remember that when they pressure you to find me.*

J.J.

"Call Hank," she demanded.

I licked my lips. "Why? What can he do?"

I waited for her answer.

"He needs to know. Are you all right?"

"No, I'm not all right. I'm angry and scared," I whispered.

I reached down and laid my hand on Bobby Lee's side, which was moving slowly up and down with each breath while he slept. I was rewarded with a half thump of his tail but he didn't open his eyes.

I took a deep breath. "Get Donnie Ray and tell him that I need him and Wayne pronto."

She headed out and I called Hank.

"Cribbs."

"It's me again, I just opened the mail. I have a note from Jimmy Joe Lane. He paid me an after-hours visit last night. Seems he toured the kennel with Bobby Lee as his guide."

"Any proof of his visit?"

"Nothing provable. Bobby Lee's leads were coiled neatly on the floor in the middle of the grooming room this morning."

"That gained your undivided attention, I bet!"

"You got that right," I said wearily.

"Don't handle the note any more than you already

have. I'll be there within the hour."

"Do you have a mug shot of him? I need one to show the crew so they know who to watch for."

"I'll get one from the prison and bring it with me."

"Thanks, Hank."

I stared out at the late-morning sunshine and realized that I had to return to the siege mentality and replace the security gates and pressure plates, and electrify the fences I had used when Bubba was stalking me. I was just getting used to the freedom from raucous alarms. It didn't seem fair, but what other choice did I have? I had discovered at the age of ten that life isn't always fair. It's just that sometimes I forget that fact.

There is a very slim line between unrequited love and vicious hate. Jimmy Joe had alluded to the safety of my dogs from the get go. I couldn't let him roam freely over my property. His admiration could become vindictive quickly. I also realized that I couldn't just sit on the sidelines and not get involved.

I couldn't understand his actions. He seemed to want me to search for him. Maybe he wanted to pit his abilities of escape against my trying to find him. Who knew what made him tick? All the years of being confined had to have molded his personality in many different ways from the simple swamp-loving teenager of long ago.

I could feel empathy for that boy and still be aware that the current Jimmy Joe could be a formidable threat to my animals and me. Defense was not enough; we would also have to go to offense.

Wayne and Donnie Ray rushed in with a hasty knock and questioning expressions, Jasmine right behind them.

"Well, we have problems." I explained about Jimmy Joe's visit.

"Hank is coming out and bringing a photograph. Run off copies and make sure all the trainers have a copy to study. Jasmine is going to call the security people and get our fences and alarms back. I don't know how long it will take them to reinstall the equipment, but until it's in place, we'll have to set up night watches. I don't think we have to worry about him in the daytime, just at night. He's a wanted man. We do, however, have to be vigilant at all times. Any questions?"

A subdued Wayne and Donnie Ray left to resume work and Jasmine took my address book back to the bedroom to call United Security.

Bobby Lee awoke and edged closer to lean against my leg. I spoke softly as I caressed his ears.

"Some watchdog you are, greeting the enemy and giving him the grand tour."

Bloodhounds are so gentle and loving. My heart swelled with love as I fretted for his safety and that of all the animals under my roof.

Jasmine returned and handed me my address book.

"I lucked out and got to speak to one of the installers. He started to give me a date for a week from now, but I told him that if it was installed by tomorrow at six P.M. you would pay the installer a personal bonus of a hundred bucks. He jumped on it and promised to deliver. Was that all right?"

"Good thinking. We're spread too thin already. We can't afford losing sleep for a week."

13
"A Stroll in the Swamp"
August 27, Tuesday, Noon

When Hank arrived, he entered quickly, and wasn't smiling. He handed me Jimmy Joe's mug shot and spoke tersely.

"Borrow your phone? We have a call out. I have to get details."

"When it rains, it pours," I mumbled, and sat waiting quietly while he spoke with the dispatcher.

Jasmine signed that she was making lunch and disappeared. I could hear Hank's side of the conversation and recognized the name and knew where we were going.

Hiram Burton, seventy-seven, and his wife, Beulah, seventy-three, lived in a small isolated farmhouse about ten miles out of Balsa City on one of the many dirt roads that wound around the edge of the Okefenokee Swamp.

He was the sole caregiver of his wife of fifty-five years who suffered from dementia first caused by a stroke, ten years in the past, then a gentle slide into feeble-mindedness and chronic confusion caused by the worsening dementia. Her body still worked, but her mind was gone. He bathed her, fed her, and watched her constantly.

Their kids begged him to place her in a nursing home but he wouldn't hear of it. She wandered off occasionally even though he was ever vigilant. Last year we were called in and I found her a short way from the house, sitting peacefully on a creek bank staring at the water.

I hoped it would be a repeat performance. I admired Hiram; he firmly practiced and believed his marriage vows from all those many years ago. Till death do us part.

I stuck my head in the kitchen and saw that Jasmine had sliced ham and was assembling sandwiches. I picked up one with mustard and Swiss cheese.

"I'm taking Gulliver. It's a seventy-three-year-old female who wanders mindlessly away from home. Who do you wish to use?"

She stared over my shoulder, considering.

"Ramona, I think."

I nodded acceptance because I had just taken a large bite of the sandwich and headed to the bedroom since Hank was still on the phone. I called Donnie Ray, and when he answered told him to load up my van with Gulliver and Ramona, that Jasmine and I would travel together.

When I came back to the kitchen with extra socks, another pair of shoes, and a bandanna, Jasmine had left to change clothes and Hank was sitting at the kitchen table eating a sandwich and drinking iced tea.

"Ready?" he mumbled with his mouth full.

"Donnie's loading the van. It'll take a few minutes."

I picked up the sack of sandwiches and headed to the back porch.

Rudy was pacing the wide planks, tail twitching with indignation and giving Bobby Lee malignant glances as he emitted small sounds of protest.

Old Faithful was patiently and hopefully waiting with both leashes clutched in his slobbering jaws.

"Ah, Bobby Lee," I crooned, feeling awful. "Not this time. No, no."

I worked on my gloves and gently removed the leads and put them back on their nails. Avoiding his eyes, I knelt and hugged his neck. "Forgive me?"

"Why don't you let him go?" Hank asked as he closed the screen door. He was holding his half-eaten sandwich.

"He's supposed to be your best dog in the kennel, if not the whole world, to hear you tell it. You never take him into the swamp anymore. Won't he get rusty or lose his edge or something if you don't let him keep in practice? You know this search is a stroll. How far can a seventy-three-year-old woman travel? Look at him. He's crushed."

"I'm taking Gulliver," I replied evenly.

I glanced Hank's way and saw his eyes widen.

"You're afraid he'll get hurt! I'll be damned. You're protecting him! How come?"

Jasmine, hurrying up the steps to help me load, saved me from an explanation. I ignored his question and took the wheel when Donnie Ray pulled the van even with the back gate.

Hank turned his unit in front of us with a screech of tires and activated the siren and flashers.

"I wish he wouldn't do that," I said waspishly. "It gives me a headache!"

"What were you two discussing when I arrived?"

"He wanted to know why I wasn't taking Bobby Lee," I admitted.

"And you said . . . ?"

"Don't *you* start."

"Forget I asked."

"All my dogs are great and I love them dearly, but Bobby Lee is special. I lost him once because of the trial and it was months before I won back his trust. I couldn't stand it if anything happened to him. After Jimmy Joe's visit and his knowing that Bobby Lee lives in the house, he must be aware that I think he's special. Jimmy Joe said he read all the press on my career, so he also knows that Bobby Lee was sightless for most of his life. I won't put him in jeopardy."

"Life is a crap shoot, Jo Beth. You can't always hedge your bets."

"I'm gonna damn sure try," I said with determination. "And that's a surprising observation from a devout Southern Christian lady like yourself."

She answered with a warm smile and a wink of conspiracy. "It's just you and me, kid."

I laughed at her nonsense. "I read an article a few days ago that I've been meaning to discuss with you," I said, changing the subject. "I want to check it out today. It's called the theory of the dominant hand."

"I'm all ears."

"Basically it's to help you guide the man-trailing dog when a trail forks and the dog is having trouble picking up the scent.

"A person panicked, running on instinct alone, and not familiar with the terrain will choose to turn in the direction of the dominant hand. Thus we now have another question to ask when we are in pursuit, whether the victim is right-handed or left-handed.

"A right-handed person will turn to the right, and a left-handed person will turn to the left. This is not a scientific theory, but it appears to work time and time again. The choice is made unconsciously. It seems that if the subject decides to backtrack, the same scenario applies—they turn right or left, according to their dominant hand."

"It sounds reasonable."

"This should help when the scent is blown all over the landscape in high winds. Might cut down on the search time."

"Do you think that she'll be difficult to find?"

"Her name is Beulah and her mind is completely gone. Her seventy-seven-year-old husband is her sole health provider and does a very good job, but no one can watch a person twenty-four hours out of a twenty-four-hour day, day in and day out. It's impossible. I admire the old man and his devotion, especially since she doesn't know him from Adam's house cat and isn't aware of his sacrifice. Their children pressed to put her in a nursing home last year, and even if we do find her and she's okay, I'm afraid they will prevail this time. If she's sent to a home, it will probably finish both of them. His only reason for getting up each morning is to take care of her."

"Will we both start out together?"

"If my memory is correct, the undergrowth is heavy around the creek, but there's a narrow trail that's fairly accessible, with lots of twists and turns following the curve of the stream. I'll start out and you can follow on an independent trail about ten minutes later."

"What was the weather report this morning?"

"Sixty percent possibility of scattered showers this afternoon and tonight. That deluge we got yesterday at the funeral didn't make it this far east. Look at the road."

I had slowed my speed and let Hank get almost out of sight so we wouldn't be eating his dust. We were bone dry in this neck of the woods and the dust swirls generated by his fast driving were taking long seconds to clear from the air.

Jasmine searched the sky for smoke. "The wind seems to be coming out of the north. How are the wildfires across the line, in Florida?"

"The small one has been contained, but the one in the southern portion of the swamp has now consumed over forty thousand acres."

"They say that's good for the swamp, renews the forest, but I always worry about the wildlife."

"The animals love the new young green shoots that come up after a fire, but I worry about the firefighters who are trying to contain the perimeters, putting out hot spots, and nuts like us who tromp through the brush during afternoon thunderstorms that generate lightning strikes."

"Have you ever been near a forest fire?"

"Not even close, thank the Lord, nor do I ever wish to be. Fire can move faster than I can run."

Hank wasn't in sight when I slowed for the turn onto a narrow dirt road that led to the Barton homestead. After a mile or so, we could see the house through a clear-cut that had been planted the previous fall.

"All the acreage around the house has been leveled since last year. It was old growth. Lumber prices have gone through the roof during the past eighteen months. The pulp mills are running double shifts."

Hank was out of his unit and standing on the front porch of the small frame house that squatted at the edge of the swamp on a shallow lot of hard-packed clay. Not one blade of grass marred the cleared area. It was swept clean with a homemade broom of dried sage grass. Mr. Hiram still practiced a lot of the old ways of living, before we became so dependent on mechanical devices.

An ancient, battered truck was under an open-sided shed that leaned precariously to the right. Its appearance was deceptive. Most people would decide it was an accident waiting to happen, but he knew it would still be standing long after he was gone. He'd probably built it himself sixty or more years ago.

Three modern cars were parked haphazardly in front of the porch. The two sons and daughter had arrived before us. I had thought that Mr. Hiram was lucky because his three children lived in the same small town where they'd been raised, until last year. I met them then after my search for their mother, when I returned her. They were outraged and shocked and disgusted with their father for not taking their advice and putting their mother into a nursing home. I had secretly wondered if Mr. Hiram considered them a blessing or a curse. I'm not a parent, and don't have any living parents, so I tried not to judge their actions too harshly.

I pulled up, shut off the motor, and sighed.

"You want to fill me in?" Jasmine was eyeing the three people who were standing facing the front-porch swing where Mr. Hiram sat slumped with his head resting in his hands.

"They are the we-told-you-so and we-knew-you-couldn't-handle-it contingent, the children, bless their nit-picking, narrow-minded little hearts."

"Since they seem to be between forty and fifty, the term 'children' doesn't seem appropriate somehow. I have discerned two thoughts from the looks that they are directing our way. They seem to feel toward you exactly the same way you feel about them, and they don't cotton to black folk."

"Let's suit up and go let them get it out of their systems. Maybe they'll feel better after. I'm trying to remember that they are worried about their mother."

We donned our rescue suits and helped each other with our snake leggings. Unloading the dogs, we attached their leads to the side of the van.

Silently we mounted the single step to the porch and waited for Hank to make the introductions. Mrs. Phelps, the female of the trio, could hardly wait until Hank finished speaking.

"What's *she* doing here?" she asked Hank, motioning Jasmine's way so no one would have any doubt about who she was discussing.

"Jasmine has come to help me search for your lost mama," I replied softly. "Wasn't that nice of her?"

"I was speaking to Sheriff Cribbs!" She was keeping her eyes on Hank and hadn't turned to face me.

"Mrs. Phelps, Ms. Jones is a qualified and certified

member of the Dunston County Search-and-Rescue team under contract with the Dunston County Sheriff's Department. Without her assistance, I'm sure Ms. Sidden would have to call off the search attempt. Do you have an objection?"

Hank's voice had been reasonable and pleasant, but I'm sure that everyone within hearing range had gotten the message that he was very displeased with Mrs. Phelps's ill-advised question. She glanced at her brothers and quickly entered the house without speaking.

I drew up a straight-backed chair with an ancient cowhide-covered seat and sat gingerly on its uneven surface, facing Mr. Hiram.

"Mr. Hiram? I'm Jo Beth Sidden. I found your wife last year down near the creek. Do you remember?"

He raised his ravaged countenance and searched my face.

"Will you find her?" His voice was barely above a whisper.

"I'll find her, I promise. Do you know when she left?"

"She seemed tired about eleven or so, she was hurting with her arthritis something awful last night. I figured that she would sleep a couple of hours since I gave her one of her pills to relax her." He hung his head in shame. "I didn't mean to fall asleep, I just laid down beside her to keep her company. I woke up at twelve and she was gone."

He looked so miserable I clasped his folded hands and raised my voice.

"It wasn't your fault, so don't go blaming yourself. Is Miz Beulah right- or left-handed?"

"What does that have to do with trying to find her?" the elder son blurted out. "Why aren't you out there looking for her instead of asking asinine questions?" His hand was in his pocket nervously jingling his loose change and the noise was annoying. I glanced at Hank and ignored him.

Hiram Burton scratched his head. "Well, that's a hard question to answer, and I'll have to do some explaining to you. Back when Beulah and I were very young, it was thought to be unlucky, at best, if you wrote with your left hand, and some even thought that it was the sign of demon possession. Beulah said that as soon as she could make a fist and hold a pencil or crayon everyone would move it from her left hand to her right and fuss at her to boot. When she started school, the teachers did the same thing. She said it was easier for her to learn how to use her right hand when someone was around, so she did everything amper, ampher, I can't recall the word I'm trying to say . . . ."

"Ambidextrous," I supplied.

"Yes'm. She could use either one."

The first time I wanted to try the dominant hand and I had to hit a snag. Since I didn't know which was really the dominant hand, it was no help.

"That's a big help," I fibbed to make him feel better. "Do you have two objects that she's worn or handled often that haven't been washed?"

"I didn't know you needed two. I brought one of her house slippers. I picked it up like you showed me last year, with a pair of kitchen tongs. I'll go get the other one."

He left, walking purposefully to get it. He wanted to help so badly because he blamed himself for letting her slip away. I heard Hank in the background getting rid of both sons, herding them inside the house and out of my hair.

14
"Gulliver's Nose at Work"
August 27, Tuesday, 1:35 P.M.

Jasmine and I stood silently waiting for Mr. Hiram to return with Beulah's slippers. His step returning was a little faster than his pace in leaving had been. He allowed a brief smile to flit across his saddened features.

"She changed from her slippers to her Indian moccasins. She knows not to wear her bedroom slippers outside. Since . . . her illness, she likes bright colors. The shoes she's wearing are bright red with colored beads."

He seemed heartened that she had remembered to change shoes before she went outside, but all I could wonder was if she also remembered that she was breaking the rules by leaving without him in attendance. I pictured a seventy-three-year-old Dorothy with thin silver-colored braids, in a faded housedress, pale legs roped with varicose veins flashing between hemline and red flats. The road she was traveling was not yellow brick but moist peat in an overgrown swamp with hidden monsters. I suppressed a shudder.

The bedroom scuffs were washable, pink cotton fleece and were excellent scent articles. He had carried them correctly with the kitchen tongs inserted inside each toe.

"Do you remember how long she's worn them?"

"Last night since about five P.M. and until eleven today. She has . . . accidents and I rotate four pairs."

"Does she slip them on and off herself?" I hoped they weren't too contaminated with his scent. It might confuse the dogs.

"She dresses herself," he said proudly, "most times." He was trying to be completely truthful.

I mentally complimented Miz Beulah once again on her excellent choice of a lifetime companion. I knew that God must still make these sturdy, dependable, and dedicated men, and I felt sorry that so many of us womenfolk just didn't know how to find one.

Jasmine and I slipped the shoes into Ziploc baggies without touching them, as we hadn't put on our gloves.

At the truck, we donned our rescue suits and backpacks and unhooked the dogs and let them find a perfect bush to piddle on. The afternoon sun was hot and humid. With the air cut off, we were already sweating.

"When we pick up a scent, Gulliver and I'll leave first," I told Jasmine. "When we're out of sight, I'll do a radio check. Wait ten minutes and start Ramona. If we have any divergent trails, check in and we can see if we're both on the same track."

We both lowered our front zippers and untied the bandannas that we had placed around our waists when we'd dressed at home, placed them in a baggie, and exchanged them. This was a precaution that we used when we ran two different trails. We never used ourselves for scent work at the kennels, and now had a scent item of each other's so that if one of us got lost or hurt, the other would have a way of tracking.

When you placed bloodhounds on a scent, it sometimes confused them when you had to change scent articles and begin to look for another trail. Bloodhounds were each individually trained and, just like people, had their own eccentricities and behavior patterns. At any given point in one outing, they could be clownish, showing a well-defined sense of humor, solemn, dedicated, and uninterested. The important part of training a bloodhound was understanding his or her actions or moods. This was not always easy.

Gulliver was an excellent man trailer but could also be a handful if he wasn't in a good mood. He was intelligent, but you had to keep his attention undivided. I was afraid that if I started Jasmine and Ramona directly behind him, he might take umbrage. He and I had a language problem and I wasn't a good mind reader.

I squatted in front of him and placed two pieces of dried deer jerky in the palm of my glove. This was to alert him that we were now working, and it did wonders getting his attention. He inhaled them and watched my hand intently. I unzipped the baggie and placed the opening under his nose. He took a deep sniff and stood, resolute, staring at my gloved hand.

"Seek, Gulliver. Find your man, find your man!" I spoke quickly, with animation, and sounded upbeat and excited. Without a flicker of interest, he still stood, resolute, and continued to stare at my gloved hand.

I took a deep breath. This might be a long, long afternoon. I repeated the process, giving him a bright chirpy order to "seek." No reaction. It occurred to me that he might be holding out for additional jerky. I stared at him and shoved the bag under his nose for another sniff. He still didn't move.

I sighed under my breath and tried to slip out the second handful of jerky for him without Jasmine spotting my actions. She doesn't believe in breaking routine because a dog is being stubborn. I'm the biggest sucker who trains in the kennel. Most know that they can con me with little effort. My back was to Jasmine and she was standing several yards away from us.

At the delivery of the second serving, the ham began the jiggle dance, wriggling his body in excitement and placing his big nostrils and elongated ears near the ground and getting down to business. I had been conned.

In the ten minutes I had been encased in the airless Kevlar DayGlo rescue suit, the perspiration was trickling down inside, dampening my T-shirt and jeans. It was eighty-six degrees and should peak at over ninety about five P.M., unless the predicted sixty percent chance of rain appeared. I eyed the small cirrus cloud smears floating lazily in the brilliant azure sky, from east to west, and hoped it would hold off until we could find Miz Beulah and return.

The family and Hank all stood on the front porch watching Gulliver traverse an eight-foot area back and forth with me trailing behind. He was trying to pick up the one scent that he had been trained to search for and identify, and separate it from the thousand others that were in the air and on the ground.

Even after seeing this for several years on hundreds of trails, I was still amazed by the awesome ability that had been bred into this noble bloodhound breed, and their enduring trait of following where their noses led them until they dropped. Owners and trainers fed them, cared for them, gave them rules of conduct. Then we could only follow along behind and let them do the work and perform their magic.

We went around the shrubbery close to the house and turned west, going toward the rear of the house, turned again, and stopped at the small screened porch at the rear. Gulliver traveled up two steps as I held the screen door open for his passage. He inspected the back door, the floor, and smelled the wooden rockers before he turned and indicated he wanted to go back outside.

He headed toward the listing shed that housed the ancient truck and circled the old shelves of tools stored in the center of the small building. Back out in the open under the hot sun, he headed east and followed the bushes planted near the house, going back to the low, open front porch where our former audience could now see us and our progress.

He was so intent on his search that he didn't detour over to greet Ramona, who was stretched out taking a nap under a small live oak shade tree, and Jasmine, who was leaning patiently against its trunk. I was proud of him. Some man-trailers will lose their concentration and occasionally stop and smell the roses or any other interesting scent that appears.

Gulliver headed up the front porch, and everyone scattered as he ignored them and sniffed the screen door and inspected the porch swing where Mr. Hiram was now sitting. I saw the old man starting to move his hand to pat Gulliver and then reluctantly stop the motion when he remembered that he might break the dog's concentration.

Last year when Ashley and I had slowly guided back a bewildered Miz Beulah from her impromptu trip to the creek, Hiram had hugged his wife and then dropped to his knees and also hugged Ashley, tears in his eyes. I sincerely hoped that Gulliver would be able to earn his hug this afternoon if we could safely return with Miz Beulah.

I had mentioned at the time of the previous search that I hadn't seen a yard dog and that our local SPCA had several appropriate candidates on hand. Being on the board, I was always seeking good homes for our unfortunate detainees and heard the longing in his reluctant refusal. I knew it was either the cost of upkeep or thinking he could not spend any time away from the care of his wife, so I didn't question it.

Mrs. Phelps, the daughter, gave a quick squeak of alarm when Gulliver smelled her shoes, and danced back mumbling her discontent.

"The animal is wasting time! He acts like he doesn't know what he's doing!"

I gave her an angry glance and kept my mouth shut. I knew she was upset, but she wasn't worthy of any explanation about Gulliver's methods. I'd let Hank cure her ignorance about the search if he so desired. Gulliver went back down the steps and we started around the house for the second time, on the same path we had taken earlier.

I knew the day was slipping away in the afternoon sunshine, but you can't rush a bloodhound's nose. I followed Gulliver as he was heading again for the backyard and lifted my gaze to the edge of the clearing. There was a narrow path there that led to the creek where we had found her last year.

Gulliver stopped so suddenly, just when I had taken my eyes off him, and turned so quickly, he almost ran into me in reversing his forward motion. I danced out of his way as he hurried by, hesitated for a heartbeat, and took a new direction that headed directly toward the creek path. His tail was high and rigid. His body stance became taller and his pace increased. I trotted behind him with quickening breaths of tentative optimism. He seemed to be locked onto a viable man-trailing scent.

When Gulliver was fully committed to the creek path, and we were several yards into the swamp and out of the line of sight, I pulled him off the scent on a temporary halt for a radio check.

"Rescue One to base. Rescue One to base. Do you read me? Over."

Hank answered. "Base to Rescue One. I read you loud and clear. Over."

"Rescue One to base. Gulliver has chosen the creek path on the east side of the house and seems to be on a good trail. I'll call Rescue Two and give instructions. If I can't reach her, call me back. Over and out."

"Rescue One to Rescue Two. Do you read me? Over."

"Rescue Two to Rescue One. I read you loud and clear. Over." Jasmine's transmission was also clear.

"Rescue One to Rescue Two, take the creek path on the east side. If I cross a path and turn, I will call it in. If you make a choice without hearing from me, keep track and call it in. Give me a ten-minute start. Over."

"Rescue Two to Rescue One. Read you five by five. Over and out."

Well, we were off to a promising start. All the radios worked so far. Communications were sometimes iffy here in the dense old growth of thick, towering trees, low areas of boggy sloughs, and the high banks on the Sewanee River and its many fingers of creeks that meandered throughout the entire swamp area. I checked the time and it was now almost four P.M. I knew we would find the creek soon, and didn't need to dig out Gulliver's water dish, but I unhooked a canteen and took a deep drink of clear town water. The creek water wouldn't hurt me but I shied away from the tea-colored water that sometimes had diminutive additives that I couldn't identify.

I started Gulliver back on his trail with the command, "Find your man, find your man." We feminists only used correct sex titles when it wouldn't confuse the bloodhounds. More men got lost out here than women, and the bloodhounds didn't seem to recognize human gender, only their own breed's sex when they were feeling randy or in love.

15
"Shit Happens"
August 27, Tuesday, 4:00 P.M.

The narrow trail's surface was a mixture of peat and clay and mud, much of it covered with pine needles, pine cones, oak and bay leaves, and windblown moss. The moist morass made a slippery surface for walking. I noticed that in the year past, since I had last walked this way on the first rescue, that the path had narrowed and was being closed with new growth pushing through the ground. Young pine saplings, along with oak and blackthorn shoots, were struggling to establish roots.

Mr. Hiram's heirs obviously didn't come this way to the creek to fish and swim too often, and I imagined that his walks with a fishing pole and Miz Beulah had been sadly curtailed. This path would be lost in another couple of years without being hacked back and cleared.

Gulliver was steadily forging ahead and had to wait, acting impatient when I had to apply my machete to a clinging, intruding vine blocking my way. The path had an almost solid canopy of thick boughs of pine and oak as low as two or three feet above my head and received very little sunlight. No breeze could penetrate the trees and heavy brush and the air was clammy and difficult to breathe.

The narrow passage led in a long, gradual curve to the left, and I knew this would lead me closer to the creek very soon. I couldn't remember how many other trails might cross the one I was now traveling. I estimated that

Miz Beulah had been alone now for five hours or more. I felt the need for haste but had to proceed prudently. I didn't need a twisted ankle or a bad gash on my face from thorns.

We approached our first intersection, a narrow Y that didn't noticeably slow Gulliver's progress. He went left, which I knew was the correct way to the creek. I had to halt him to inform Jasmine.

"Rescue One to Rescue Two. Rescue One to Rescue Two. Do you read? Over."

It took two more tries before I heard Jasmine's intermittent raspy response.

". . . Two to Rescue . . . Repeat. Over."

My heart sank. We couldn't be more than three or four hundred yards apart and already we were experiencing transmitting problems? I cursed the thick humidity, heavy growth, low areas, gremlins, or whatever. I finally got through on the third effort and explained the direction we'd taken.

My voice had risen considerably and my mouth was dry. I couldn't remember how much farther it was to water and Gulliver was panting. I removed my pack and dug out his water dish and emptied the balance of my first canteen. I had another full one on my belt and two emergency quarts in my pack. He lapped it up noisily and waited for more.

"That will last you because we've got creek water coming up for you soon, big guy, but I have to conserve mine. You shouldn't have cadged that second handful of jerky. It makes you thirsty."

I put him back on the trail, unconsciously blowing the

small puffs of air from my lips that kept the gnats away from my mouth and nostrils. When I'd first entered the path, I had tied a bandanna around my head to protect my ears from the dive-bombing sand flies. I now only had to wipe my face with an additional bandanna every thirty seconds to keep the rivulets of sweat from burning my eyes. Thank God we only had another two weeks or so of gnats and then they would be history until next May. This would leave only mosquitoes, horseflies, yellow flies, sand flies, honeybees, wasps, dirt daubers, and a few more varieties of insects that I have had the misfortune of meeting but never identifying. After crushing them, all I would have left to inspect would be a wet black smear.

The light was fading. I couldn't glimpse enough sky to judge if it was low thunderstorm clouds heavy with rain or just the sun easing behind the tall forest that would block the receding rays. Whatever the reason, I didn't like the coming darkness. Stumbling around in this tiny corridor with only a headlight and a flashlight was not conducive to easy walking. I was now having to watch for the almost hidden small cypress roots that can send you sprawling on your hands and knees if you trip on them. This meant we were getting closer to the water, but it was also slowing our forward progress.

Jasmine and Ramona should be joining us soon. Even though she had left minutes behind me, I had been slowed by chopping back the obstructive vines and pro-truding limbs. The path should be easier for her and they should be traveling faster. I was looking down at my feet and almost stumbled over Gulliver because he had suddenly stopped trailing and was turned sideways and sniffing at something in the clump of six-inch grass. I caught a faint odor of urine and saw a small pile of feces and some faint stains on a handful of pulled up grass. Miz Beulah had made a rest stop.

I stood there worrying about her running into the numerous vines that had tried to claw me on our trip. She might not know how to or couldn't avoid them, and if she was scratched, the cuts could become septic in a short time in this heat. I also belatedly remembered that I hadn't questioned Mr. Hiram very carefully about her health problems. I felt a pang of guilt. She could have adult onset diabetes, and if so, by now might be hypoglycemic. Nothing was mentioned about insulin, but many people take a couple of pills a day and are supposed to watch their diets but don't consider themselves as having a disease. I tried to find comfort in the fact that Mr. Hiram took excellent care of her and would have mentioned the illness, hopefully. However, he was also upset and feeling guilty about her slipping away and might have temporarily forgotten. Diabetes could exacerbate any infection. I also remembered the thin moccasins that covered her feet.

I was surprised when Gulliver turned and headed back toward me. His stance was rigid and his expression seemed intensified as he nosed around tracking the scent. He was going over the same ground that we had just passed.

"Hey, Gulliver? What's happening?"

I was working him on the six-foot lead, as we didn't have much room and he always wanted to move like a freight train. I tugged him backward and finally stopped him.

"Why would she turn around here?" I asked him, confused. "She was heading toward the creek. Let's try it again a little farther along this trail, before we backtrack. We know she couldn't have made it turning off the path. She couldn't have moved three feet through the heavy brush."

Gulliver didn't seem impressed with my reasoning, but I got him to turn around, reluctantly, and head in our original direction. I should have known better than to argue with his gifted nose. Less than fifteen feet of his casting back and forth and humming a low, frustrated whine, he pulled up short and stood slouched, then turned his head in my direction looking lost and uncertain.

I peered ahead of him and saw the reason. The path had simply petered out. All that was in front of us were heavy vines, a thick growth of gallberry bushes, and solid trees several years old. A dead end. It was that time of day when the natural light was muted, and too soon for a flashlight or headlamp. I stooped and patted Gulliver's head and rubbed his ears.

"I should have known your nose is better than my guesses. You are a great man trailer and I'm a klutz. Shall we turn around?"

A few yards back down the trail, we heard Jasmine and Ramona seconds before we saw them making their way toward us.

"Are you all right?" Jasmine called out anxiously.

"Fine. We're just lost, like you two."

Gulliver and Ramona greeted each other like long-lost relatives. They twisted their short leads together and whined and smelled each other with delight.

"Let's take a break," I suggested and slumped against a raised mound at the base of a gnarled water-oak trunk. Jasmine took a moment to inspect a safe area and slid down near me.

Jasmine's face looked drawn in the subdued light.

"You look tired."

"I'm sitting too long in too many classes trying to finish my second year. And the heat is getting to me. I'm cutting down next month. I've already filled out my schedule for fall."

"Great. Rosie's offered to take two of our regular search visits each week, and I'm not taking any more new contracts until we can get another trainer who can handle Rosie's and your overflow. It's too much for both of you."

"Why are we lost? Did Gulliver lose the scent?"

"Gulliver and I agree that she must have doubled back. This path dead-ends a few yards behind us. With her traveling this area twice, it made the trail easier to scent. My guess is that she took the right path back at the Y crossing and Gulliver failed to catch it, or she decided to step off this path on her way back and take a shortcut through this monstrous growth. She has fifty years of memories of this land in her confused mind. I don't have any idea what she might think of next. I didn't notice anywhere she could have left the trail coming in, but I wasn't checking it too closely because Gulliver was confidently covering ground on the path.

If she decided to blaze her own way to the creek, I'll tell you true, we're in a whole heap of trouble."

"So now we slow down and check both sides of this trail on the way back . . . with lights," she added.

"That's the plan," I said with a sigh. "You take the left, and I'll check the right side."

Standing, I stretched and we both starting untangling the dogs' leads. We took out headlamps, and adjusted them to shine straight in front of where we looked. I held my lead in my left hand, and carried the five cell in my right. It had a wider beam and was worth carrying the extra weight. Thick, dark green foliage with black shadows absorbed the light and reflected an unwavering wall of gloom. I occasionally clenched my eyes then stretched them wider to try to achieve better night vision. It didn't seem to help much.

Gulliver was impatient with the slower pace and kept trying to pull ahead. He was following a strong trail and couldn't understand why we were stopping so often to check the bushes. He kept glancing back at Ramona and Jasmine, working behind him. He started a soft whine of discontent.

"Take it easy, Gulliver, we want to make sure. Slow down, ease off." I repeated the refrain often to reassure him that he was doing a good job.

My left arm began to ache from the strain. I couldn't switch hands while using the flashlight because it was too awkward. I was forced to tie my extra bandanna around my forehead. It was too much effort to keep swiping my eyes with the hand that held the flashlight. After twenty minutes I called a halt, pulled Gulliver off the scent, and walked back to Jasmine.

"Let's change sides. My left arm is killing me. He keeps pulling ahead."

I moved to the left, and it seemed to rest my left hand. Gulliver was still straining ahead. He surely didn't appreciate the slow pace and I almost missed the small opening in the bushes. My light raked over it and I had only a nanosecond vision of a small tunnel, then the unbroken brush returned.

I pulled up on Gulliver's lead and walked back several steps. Ramona and Jasmine joined us and we both investigated the narrow opening with our lights while the dogs wriggled with impatience. Ramona pushed forward and lowered her nose first. Gulliver stood still and watched her work.

"It looks like a deer, or a small-animal trail," I said hopefully. No way did I want to stoop or crawl through the heavy brush after dark.

"Ramona wants to go in. What do you think?" Jasmine asked while leaning over and peering into the dark slit, holding firmly to Ramona's leash.

I sighed with disappointment. "Then we try it. I'll be right behind you. Be careful."

Snakes crawled freely and fed in early darkness and early morning. A full cast of wild creatures lived in this environment and moved around this swamp in a two-hour cycle of forage and resting. I had no desire to meet any of them on a night trail in thick brush while stooping or crawling.

16
"A Less Than Perfect Rescue"
August 27, Tuesday, 7:30 P.M.

Can you stand up?" I called, more to keep voice contact than to get information. I didn't like Ramona and Jasmine disappearing in the darkness and not knowing what they were doing.

"So far," Jasmine answered, her voice already subdued by the thickness of the surrounding foliage.

I was hovering so close that I was bending over Gulliver, trying to walk by his side instead of staying behind him. After an interminable wait of thirty seconds, I called again.

"What's happening?"

"Nothing so far," she said, sounding a tad testy. "Do you want to lead? I think we still have room enough to change places here."

"No, no," I yelled quickly, "just checking that you're all right."

"Well . . . if you're sure."

I bit my lip and told myself to shut up. It would seem as if I didn't trust her to lead if I kept up a running dialogue of questions. I wasn't used to being second on a trail. In fact, I couldn't remember an instance when I hadn't been behind the lead man trailer. This time I managed to stay silent a full five minutes.

"Does it seem that Ramona is on a viable scent?"

When she didn't immediately answer, I quickly surged forward and almost stepped on her. She was

125

squatting in the path with her hand guarding her eyes to keep me from destroying her night vision with my light.

"You rang?" Her tone was wry.

"Sorry, I'm just nervous. We've used up a lot of time. I know it's a cold trail. Just checking."

"You're having an anxiety attack because you're not leading the pack. I would suggest that you and Gulliver take the lead and we'll all feel better. What do you say?"

"Are you sure? It's not that I don't trust you . . ."

"Believe me, Jo Beth, Ramona and I will be much better off ten paces to the rear. Trust me on this. Move past, please."

I turned my light on the narrow sides of the opening and sucked in a startled breath.

"What in God's name is all this?"

My light was not penetrating more than a foot on either side of the narrow trail. I gaped in wonder at the solid wall of vegetation hemming in our clearance and the tiny opening we had to advance into.

"You mean this?" She was pointing around at the morass on all sides of her. Her voice rose, light and chirpy. "This is the new growth of Chinese tallow trees. They are indigenous to China and were imported in the nineteen thirties and planted in the South Florida Everglades to keep the topsoil from eroding away. For the past sixty years or so, they've been traveling north and infesting hundreds of thousands of acres. I've read that they're hardy little buggers and can grow a foot a month in a wet climate. I'd judge these beauties to be about six months old. Can you imagine what they are going to look like in six years?"

I stared at the close-growing slim saplings. "Why haven't I heard about them before, and how did you know?"

"It seems our government experts said it would take a good twenty more years for them to spread into northern Florida and southern Georgia, and who begins planning twenty years in advance for a problem? Seems that some of the experts have been saying 'oops' for the past three years, as they have shown up in almost every county in north Florida. Don't you like the way they are spreading the news? I read about them about three weeks ago for the first time."

"So when is the state gonna start eradicating them?"

"Well, they have a teensy-weensy problem." She stared gloomily at the thick shoots. "The wind carries the seed. They don't have any way of stopping them."

"Nothing?"

"Not so far."

"You would think they would have learned from the kudzu vine," I said sadly. "They imported it from China and Japan." Kudzu is a climbing vine that's both widespread and runs rampant in the southern United States.

"No, and we still have water hyacinths, which have taken over our lakes. They spend billions a year to kill them and we're slowly losing the battle."

I glanced around. "This is creepy. Let's get out of here."

We maneuvered around each other, keeping the dogs from tangling their leads, and I put Gulliver out front; he seemed to have no difficulty in picking up the scent. He charged forward, raring to go, and I had to keep slowing him down. He was exhibiting a lot more excitement now that he was back in the lead. I guess we both loved to hog the spotlight.

Gulliver suddenly pulled so hard that I went to my knees. I heard his raspy intake of breath and then a deep-throated bay erupt from his jaws, which was duplicated by Ramona in her next breath. They were signaling that they had found their target! I increased my forward scramble in elation and found myself suddenly jerked facedown as Gulliver's rump disappeared from view. His entire weight was pulling me into a black abyss. Before I could react, Ramona was slamming into my backside with equal force. She had apparently decided that since she couldn't go around me, she'd advance by crawling over me. We both slid over the edge of a slippery twelve-foot slope of mud. I had no idea what was happening to the others, but I hit the water of the creek headfirst, Ramona on my shoulders. I felt the water close over my head.

I came up coughing and sputtering into inky blackness. There wasn't any light, not even a faint glow of sky or a shadow of creek bank. I had dropped my flashlight, and either my headlamp had shorted out or one of the delicate wires had been stripped from the battery terminals in my pocket.

I brought both hands up to claw at my eyes, knowing I was covered in mud and green algae slime and other unpleasant things that thrived in the water. In the same breath, I realized that I still had Gulliver's lead wrapped around my right wrist and the absence of any light meant that Jasmine had suffered the same fate and was in the water.

"Jasmine!" I yelled. "Jasmine, can you hear me?"

Yelling made my ears pop and I heard heavy thrashing sounds near me in the water. At the same time I yelled for her, I began to haul in Gulliver's lead. My heart started pounding from anxiety.

"Jasmine!"

"I'm here," she answered calmly. She sounded quite near. "I have Ramona's leash. Do you have Gulliver's?"

"Yes," I said, trying to keep my voice low. "Watch out for the dogs. They just might decide to hitchhike a ride on your head."

Each dog weighed more than 120 pounds. Of course, they both could easily dog-paddle until we hauled them out, but if the darkness or suddenness of the situation made them panic, they could be potentially dangerous adversaries.

Before I could locate Gulliver's head in the water I felt a nudge on my right shoulder. I shot up a foot out of the water before Jasmine spoke.

"It's me. The bank is on your left. We've drifted a short way with the current. We should swim back about ten feet. Do you need any help?"

"Of course not," I said quickly, trying to sound calm and collected. How was she able to see so well in this pitch-black darkness? My eyes weren't giving me a clue and I barely knew which end was up. I ran my soggy gloves down Gulliver's lead until I felt his wet fur and collar. I was already churning the water in the direction she'd given me but it was strictly on faith. I couldn't see shit. My ears gave another pop and I heard Gulliver's energetic grunts before I felt his hot breath near my right cheek.

"As soon as your feet touch bottom or you get a grip on the bank, we have to get rid of these packs. We have two to three minutes of buoyancy before the water seeps in. After that they'll pull us down like thirty-pound stones."

"We're almost there," Jasmine replied. I didn't hear any tension in her voice or any heavy breathing. Course she was six years younger than me and hadn't smoked like a chimney for twelve years like I had, but it still got to me. I tried taking slower breaths and decided to cut my pizza intake to only twice a week.

My feet settled in the blessed soft mud. I unhooked my backpack and wiggled free. I almost lost my footing as I tried to sling it upward at the moment Gulliver's paws connected with the barely discernable creek bank. I teetered awkwardly and felt Jasmine steady me from behind. I placed both of my hands under Gulliver's rump and shoved him up the canted slope. We were both slipping and sliding but finally made it to the top. I rolled over on my back gasping like a gaffed fish while trying to rake from my face the thick mud that Gulliver had dislodged in his energetic scrabble to freedom. He stood straddling my body and shook water from his fur, then began to whine and try to lick my face. I gave him a feeble push to get him off me.

"We both are out of shape," Jasmine said mildly from my right.

"Perish the thought," I uttered dryly. "I'm suffering and now is not the time to lecture. I've already promised myself to halve my pizza consumption and I don't feel like giving up anything else."

I sensed and heard movement beside me as I turned my head and stared in her direction, seeing faint shadows in motion and two dogs wriggling in unison.

"Do you think our spare flashlights will work? They are supposed to be waterproof." She must be digging into her backpack. I couldn't continue to lie here like a beached whale. I wearily pushed myself upright and began to grope around for mine. I had no idea where it was.

"Aha!" she called as a narrow beam of light stabbed into the ground from a height of six inches. She had pointed it at the ground so she wouldn't rob us of our night vision.

"Well, it's better than a candle or a flickering match, that is, if we have any dry."

She shined the light on my backpack as I dug around and searched through wet lumps and packages for mine. I palmed it and aimed it at the muddy bank, clicking the switch several times with no success.

"Christ!" I yelled with frustration as I hit it sharply with my fist and then shook it.

Jasmine raised her light high enough that she could take in my sodden hair still dripping water onto the shoulders of my waterproof Kevlar rescue suit. That is, I would have remained dry inside if I hadn't gone into the water ass over teakettle, on my face, and become totally submerged. From the clammy and squishy feeling of my clothing, I knew I was soaked to the skin from the water that had leaked in around my neckline.

"I know this is a bad time to impart some news, but I think I know why my light works and yours doesn't."

"Yes?" I suddenly had a premonition that I knew what she was going to say before she could tell me.

"I slid in feet first and was able to keep myself upright when I entered the water."

"Yeah?"

She took the flashlight and moved it slowly up her body until the beam highlighted her face and hair. Both were clean and dry. "Ta da!" she said with a flourish.

"That is sooo . . . like you!" I was giggling and had to push each syllable out independently.

Jasmine grimaced and moved the light from her face. "We haven't mentioned the dogs baying and sliding in the water. She's in the creek, isn't she?"

"Looks that way," I said sadly. "We'll have to come back at daylight with the cadaver dogs." I sighed. "Let's get these dogs unwound from their leashes and call Hank."

I stood up and mentally groaned. My socks and shoes were sopping. I'd have blisters the size of quarters before we got back. I had extra socks but no extra shoes. My only comfort was in thinking that Jasmine would suffer right along with me. After all, she went in *feet* first.

The dogs were excited that we were moving. Jasmine held the light as I untangled the leads.

"Jo Beth!" Jasmine called plaintively as both Gulliver and Ramona took off, choosing the most direct passage, which was right between her legs. She fell to the right with the only light and I tightened my grip in time to keep from losing my hold on both of them.

"Are you all right?" The light was on the ground, pointing away from her. It was all I could do to hold on to the impatient dogs.

"I'm fine. The only thing wounded is my dignity."

At that moment both of them began baying. She retrieved the light and yelled in my ear.

"What's going on?"

"They want to go parallel on the creek bank! Looks like we may be wrong about Miz Beulah being in the water!"

Even though she couldn't see me, I was grinning from ear to ear.

17
"Cheating the Grim Reaper"
August 27, Tuesday, 9:00 P.M.

Jasmine ran to take Ramona's lead, as I had my hands full with both of the dogs straining and struggling to move forward. Our only light was a focused narrow beam that was far from adequate for one, much less two handlers. On a search, bloodhounds run mute. They only start baying when they are sure their target is near. Sliding into the creek had dampened their enthusiastic bays and temporarily confused them, but now they were back on track and wanted their reward.

We got them under control and Jasmine took the lead because she had the flashlight. I couldn't see a way to ask for it without looking like I didn't think she could handle the duty, so I swallowed my misgivings and kept quiet. She swung the light backward at our feet every thirty seconds or so to light our way, and I was trying to adjust to partial darkness and a brief glimpse of the trail.

My problem was that Gulliver kept right behind Jasmine's heels since he didn't particularly need to see to strain forward. All bloodhounds follow a scent with their head lowered to the ground and their eyes half hidden in the soft folds of loose skin that fall over their eyes. They concentrate so deeply on following the scent smell that an uncontrolled bloodhound would step in front of a roaring semi on a busy highway if the scent led him across the road.

I had tightened up the length of Gulliver's lead and had him so close that we were almost side by side. I bumped into him frequently and he nudged my legs just as often. I was concentrating on not losing my balance and sprawling into the brush, and on trying to ignore my wet socks rubbing blisters on the soles of my feet with each step.

Every time Jasmine and Donnie Ray and I tried to have an intelligent discussion about what we carried in our packs on searches, it was two against one. They tried to eliminate items and I tried to add. The average weight of a full backpack was thirty-two pounds. I knew that they were right, that we couldn't take everything we *might possibly* need, but I also knew that one rule I'd just made up would be gospel for me in the future. I would never leave on another search without an extra pair of shoes and two pairs of socks packed in a sealed baggie, even if I had to jettison survival food. A rumbling gut was better than inflamed feet.

A bloodhound's glorious baying has an eerie sound that startles most people when they hear it. The sound can also cause goose bumps in me even though I have heard it often, for several years. A person man trailing is thrilled to hear the good news for five minutes or so, but after that, two of them sounding off can give a seasoned handler a splitting headache. With the added stress of a night search, too little light, and burning feet, a headache can develop into a migraine. The top of my head felt like it was going to explode. I began to pray for deliverance.

Jasmine stopped her forward movement so suddenly that Gulliver and I tried to crawl up her backside. She must have braced for our assault, since we didn't succeed in toppling her.

"What?" I muttered in angst.

"She's down on the trail ahead!" Jasmine's excited response was terse because we both had our hands full trying to hold back the two celebrants from running forward to pounce on their target and nuzzle, lick, and expect their earned praise.

Unless they have been abused, bloodhounds love everyone with equal vigor—cops, robbers, visitors, and burglars—up to and including ax murderers. They don't care if they are good guys or bad guys if they can receive some love pats and caresses for their efforts.

Jasmine and I manhandled them over to nearby saplings, tied them, and hastily congratulated them on their find.

With Jasmine holding the light on Miz Beulah, we examined the scene.

"It doesn't look good." Jasmine spoke too loudly for the sudden silence. The normal night sounds of crickets, cicadas, croaking frogs, and the warning caws of crows hadn't yet returned to the stillness. The echoes of the raucous baying seemed to linger in the air.

Miz Beulah was lying with her body in a scrunched half circle, her thin arms, above her head, spanning a narrow washed-out furrow that fed run-off rainwater into the creek. It was an awkward position and looked uncomfortable.

We knelt on either side of her, and since her head was turned to my side, I held out my hand for the light. Her eyes were closed. I leaned over and placed my ear to her chest and could hear a thready heartbeat.

"She's alive!" I proclaimed as my own heart increased its pace. I put the light back on her face. Her eyes were exaggerated ovals of horror and a scream rushed from her throat with such force and depth I almost dropped the light. The piercing scream caromed and bounced in my already throbbing skull.

I quickly passed the light to Jasmine while I removed my wet gloves with my teeth. I gathered her arms from above her head and rubbed her hands between my own to warm them. All the while I was trying to reassure her with soothing explanations.

"Miz Beulah, you're safe. You're gonna be fine. Please rest. We'll have you back in your bed in no time. Listen to me, please. You'll make yourself ill if you stay excited like this. You're safe, you're safe."

My continued litany didn't ease the volume or the timing of her screams, which were as regular as a metronome.

"Any suggestions?" I said wearily to Jasmine as I kept trying to ease Miz Beulah's fears. I noticed that she had pulled off her own gloves and was tenderly rubbing Miz Beulah's brow and gently patting her shoulders.

"You're doing all I can think of," she said, trying to time her voice so I could hear her between the small silences as Miz Beulah breathed in for another Olympic emanation. "Couldn't you sedate her?"

My wry reply was heartfelt. "Don't I wish! I'm scared now to give her any narcotic. I'm afraid she might go into shock from this hysteria. I'm afraid to move her because she could have a broken back, broken pelvis, internal injuries, or whatever. She might even have a weak heart."

I could see the glitter of Jasmine's eyes in the glow of the flashlight. "In my considered opinion, she has a sound heart."

How many times have you thought of the old axiom, "If I knew then what I know now, would I have made a different decision?" We can only speculate, but at this moment, I had no idea how many times these past few lines of dialogue would repeat in my memory.

I grinned through my pain. "Take the light and your radio and call Hank from a distance where you can hear his answers. Make sure he doesn't have projection before you start discussing Miz Beulah's condition. Also tell him to keep the male heirs from wanting to rush to the rescue. We have enough on our plate without two sons bumbling around out here."

"Do you want me to set up some candles and get you a dozen aspirin before I make the call?"

"How did you know?"

"I'm psychic. Your face is green and you keep squinting your eyes."

"Better get EMTs out here first, but thanks."

She backed out of sight with the light and I sat in the darkness and suffered.

The term *projection* is a code word we use when we call to give bad news to Hank or whoever is receiving at home base during a search. The waiting relatives have a tendency to hover around the radio to listen to what is happening in the field. When Jasmine reached Hank, and if the heirs could hear, he would disconnect, move a safe distance from their hearing, and call Jasmine back. It's easier to pass on bad news without them hearing details firsthand.

She returned and squatted, leaning near my ear so I would be able to hear her. Miz Beulah wasn't showing any signs of fatigue or hoarseness. Her current scream was as full-bodied as her first. My heart went out to her in equal amounts of pity and forbearance. All I could do was hold her hand and periodically wipe her brow. She was perspiring heavily. Screaming is hard work and I couldn't believe her stamina.

"Hank has to call me back in five. Be just a second."

She brought me four aspirin, a dry paper towel from her pack, as my bandannas were soaked, and a thin thermal ground sheet that she began to tuck around our patient.

"What's the game plan?" she asked.

"Can you take both dogs out and guide in the paramedics? I hate to send you without your pack, but I may need something, and everything in mine is soaked."

"Sure. You know that without asking. I'm in better physical shape and younger than you are. Anything else?"

"Yeah, two things. I need your working radio, and you need to treat your elders better. At this moment, I feel ninety!"

I saw the flash of her white teeth as she raised her arm to her head. I couldn't hear her laughter or what she was saying to Hank as she was backing away. I hadn't even heard the shrill chirp of the radio.

She was back beside me in the next couple of minutes, and gave me a waved okay that she had reported to Hank. She lighted four six-inch tapers and stuck them in the mud and peat mixture. She laid four spare candles beside me and two emergency flares and a Ziploc baggie holding matches.

I handed her back the two flares, shaking my head negatively.

"We don't dare use these. These woods are too dry. They would light up like a tinderbox from an errant spark."

She packed them back in my backpack and leaned close.

"Anything else you need? I should be heading back. The EMTs will be here soon."

"Nothing. Take care." She turned to release Gulliver and Ramona.

"Jasmine!" I yelled. Her head swiveled in my direction.

"If you have an emergency, fire three shots with your thirty-eight. I'll find you!"

She flashed a grin and waved. I knew what she was picturing in her mind. The sight of me galloping along the trail with a candle in each fist, rushing headlong to her rescue.

What if it rained? A sobering thought. The forecast had been for a sixty-percent chance of scattered showers this afternoon and tonight. Rain could still appear, and if it did, I would have to manage. My back needed a tree to lean against but there wasn't one close enough. I wanted Miz Beulah to feel my touch and know someone was near.

I edged around until I could prop Jasmine's backpack behind me and eased my right shoulder on its bulk. I tried to ignore the throbbing in my head, Miz Beulah's primal screams, and the stinging blisters on my feet. The weak candles were drawing moths, which circled and dove in their suicide flights to self-destruction. I automatically blew out of the corners of my lips to keep the gnats, mosquitoes, and other assorted stinging insects from gnawing on my face. Because of my pre-occupation with my assorted aches and pains, it was a good ten minutes before I remembered that the need to protect the dogs' noses from aromatic odors was past. I quickly dug into Jasmine's pack and pulled out the Off. I liberally sprayed Miz Beulah's hands and my own, then rubbed more Off onto our faces. At least one aggravation was eliminated.

I removed my snake protectors and my wet shoes and placed moleskin pads over my blisters. I donned dry socks but knew that the minute I put my shoes back on, they would get wet and clingy. I sat on another thin thermal plastic sheet and let my feet get the air and remain dry as long as possible.

I sat, hurt and worried about Jasmine with two dogs and no working radio, Miz Beulah's injuries, and what I was going to do to stop Jimmy Joe's onslaught on my compound. A person shouldn't have to deal with more than one stalker in a lifetime. Bubba had filled my quota of sleepless nights. His threats were gone, with only the nightmares of my shooting him remaining. Searching the dark, eerie space surrounding me, I worried about many things.

18
"The Rescue"
August 27, Tuesday, 10:00 P.M.

In the still night with virtually no wind, I could hear the EMTs long before I could see their lights. Miz Beulah's seemingly eternal lament didn't sound as strident as when she had first begun. Either she was tiring, or the repetition had lulled me into a cocoon of forbearance, or the aspirins were working. Whatever the reason, I was grateful for the result.

Jasmine had guided the EMTs in without Ramona. It was basically only three turns, and she knew them well from trudging them twice, once in and once out. Coming back in must have seemed a snap without a thirty-two-pound backpack and a large dog straining against a lead and threatening to dislocate her shoulder. The medics were carrying two-way radios, medical supplies, and a collapsible stretcher. All she would have was her .38 special in a holster, a water bottle clipped on her belt, a flashlight with fresh batteries, and another one in her pocket for me.

It was nice to know that the dogs had been watered and fed and were now taking a well-deserved nap in their cages. When we returned, regardless of the hour, Wayne and Donnie Ray would carefully check them for ticks, give them a dry-shampoo brushing, and bed them down in their kennel. I liked to think that they were dreaming about the cheeseburger treat they always received on the way home from a search but I wasn't sure. The only thing I was positive of was the fact that when we pulled into the well-lighted area that produced such succulent smells, they would be excited and salivating.

I knew why the EMTs were so vocal. This was the routine each time we guided them into this morass. It was the equivalent of whistling in the dark. I have seen grown men whimper when they discovered they were lost, in total darkness, within the confines of this vast primeval swamp. A person who wasn't afraid and pumped full of adrenaline was stupid. There are too many pitfalls that can cause injury and incapacitation and too many critters that would scuttle away in the daylight but that will turn and charge in the night. After all, this is their territory and the night belongs to them.

I put on my shoes, folded the plastic I had been sitting on, and released Miz Beulah's hand with a final pat. I got out of the way, because I knew when they saw their patient they would be consummate professionals and go to her immediately. I also knew that they would shine their bright lights straight into my eyes upon arrival and rob me of my night vision. It never fails. I turned my back and closed my eyes in anticipation.

Jasmine said, "Hi." She stood quietly, near me.

"Any deterioration in her condition since you found her?" The first EMT voice was crisp and authoritative.

"None that I can see," I answered pleasantly. "Could you please lower your lights?" I had raised my voice so they could hear me, but as yet hadn't faced them.

"Oh, sorry." Both lights were whipped to the ground and found Miz Beulah's form.

The second voice yelled in wonder, "My God, how long has she been screaming like this? Did you scare her?"

I made the mistake of turning while I answered.

"She's been screaming steadily for a little over an hour. OH SHIT!"

Second Voice had turned his five-cell brightness flush in my face. I guess he felt he needed to see my lips move to comprehend me. I had squeezed my eyes closed a nanosecond too late. Now all I could see was white circles of brightness and black dots swimming behind closed lids.

"Move your light!" Jasmine yelled.

I had thrown up both hands to help screen my vision, but I could still discern the light fading when I heard her sharply in-drawn breath and bleat of disgust. I peeked with one eye between my fingers and saw that her face

143

was highlighted with the same bright exposure that had blinded me. I couldn't help it; it had been a long afternoon. I brayed with laughter. It took several heartbeats before Jasmine joined in.

"Jeez!" the EMT muttered, sounding insulted. "What's the big deal?"

He finally moved the light back to his patient.

"The big deal," I explained between giggles, "is that a she bear who obviously has cubs nearby has dropped by once already to protest our proximity to her lair. You have just successfully destroyed our night vision, and as far as I know, we're the only two with guns!"

The devil made me do it, it's my only excuse, that and blistered feet, skin chafing in wet clothes, and a head still reverberating with Miz Beulah's pitiful cries.

"Wha . . . where . . . which way did she go?" He was flashing his light madly in a circle, trying to see in all directions.

"Harve, for God's sake, she's putting you on!" First Voice yelled sharply. "Steady the light and help me!"

I sobered instantly. "I apologize. That was a rotten thing to do. Very unprofessional, and I'm sorry. Is there anything we can do to help?" I felt bad for kidding at a time like this.

"Just keep the she bear at bay, and we'll handle the medical procedures," First Voice pronounced crisply.

He had effectively put me in my place without raising his voice.

After a few minutes, our night vision returned, at least enough for us to help. Jasmine picked up the flickering candles, snuffed them out in the mud, and packed them in the backpack. She handed me the extra flashlight from her hip pocket. I trained it toward their working forms, hovering over them to give them effective coverage.

They had a cervical collar on Miz Beulah and had eased her on a rigid backboard and were carefully sliding her onto the stretcher. Second Voice was spreading a soft wool blanket over her tiny form and I noticed that First Voice started to discard the thin insulated plastic sheet, but had second thoughts. He tucked it over the blanket and they strapped her snugly so she couldn't move about. Her vocal protest never faltered.

First Voice was taping a small flashlight on the foot-long vertical pole that held the IV drip. They would be able to see that it was working on the trek back.

"Ready to travel if you are."

"My name is Jo Beth," I replied, holding out my hand.

"I'm Ron, and this is Harvey, or Harve." I shook hands with both of them.

"Ron, I had morphine but I was afraid to give her any."

"I gave her a mild sedative, but not enough to slow her down. I felt the same as you. Let's get her out of here."

Jasmine led the way and I brought up the rear. I put my light on the path so Ron could see and also tried to keep any vines from catching on the stretcher. Jasmine was doing the same for Harvey and herself. It took us a little more than thirty minutes on the trip back and in the last ten minutes of the trip Miz Beulah's pitiful shrieks dwindled and finally stopped. She was snoring peacefully when they loaded her in the ambulance.

Mr. Hiram thanked Jasmine and me, but the sons and daughter were too busy closing up the house and deciding who Mr. Hiram was going to ride with to the hospital to pay any attention to us.

Hank leaned against the van as we wearily loaded up.

"Can I buy you ladies a late supper?"

"I can't speak for Jasmine, but I've been wet for over two hours. All I want is a hot bath and dry clothes and maybe a slice or two of pizza."

"I'll skip the pizza. I'll settle for a hot bath while sipping a glass of white wine, then bed. I have an early morning search," Jasmine said.

"We have to stop and get Gulliver and Ramona a cheeseburger," I said.

Hank looked into my eyes.

"I'll pick up the pizza and have it on the table waiting for you when you finish your bath."

Say no, you ninny. Say you're too tired. Say you planned on staying up the rest of the night to keep an eye out for Jimmy Joe until the security gates are reinstalled. Say something.

"Don't order any anchovies for me," I replied weakly.

"Sure you don't want any, Jasmine?"

She glanced at me and then looked at Hank.

"Thanks, but no thanks. All I want is sleep."

Jasmine drove us home. I peeled out of my rescue suit and enjoyed the warm breeze blowing in the window. We stopped at a Hardee's on Highway 301, as it was the only burger joint open after ten. I looked at my watch when we pulled up at the pick-up window. It was twenty minutes till midnight.

The dogs were ecstatic. They held the burgers in their jaws for the required five seconds to prove they remembered their training not to eat until they were told it was okay. The food disappeared like magic, in two chomps.

We were almost home before Jasmine spoke.

"Are you sure you know what you're doing?"

I sighed. "It's just a pizza."

"Don't give me that," she said with a laugh. "I saw that look that passed between you two. It's been over for months and I don't want to see him hurt, again. You know that nothing would make me happier than to see you two together. This is still Tuesday for the next few minutes. *Sunday* you were furious and said you would never forgive him. Are you really, really sure?"

"No," I said honestly. "But how can I be sure? How can anyone be absolutely sure? I've been thinking about him a lot lately . . ."

Jasmine groaned.

Wayne and Donnie Ray walked out to meet us when we pulled into the courtyard. Wayne unloaded Gulliver and Ramona and Donnie Ray took the van to the shed. I told Jasmine good night; Bobby Lee and Rudy were waiting for me on the back porch.

"Hi, guys, did you miss me?" I hugged Bobby Lee and Rudy allowed me to pick him up.

"God, you weigh a ton," I whispered as I draped him over my shoulder and tickled his ribs.

I checked their water and food dishes. Wayne had fed them. Rudy tried to con me into believing that he was starving by mewing piteously.

"You're not getting a second supper. You're still three pounds overweight."

I turned on the water in the tub and dumped in my best bubble bath. I rummaged in my save-for-best lingerie drawer and found my new ice blue gown and pulled the matching silk robe out of the closet. I threw my damp clothes into the washer and did a quick tick inspection under the bright lights. I massaged in shampoo and slid into the steaming water. I rested my head on a folded towel and let my thoughts drift.

A few minutes later, after a discreet knock, Hank cracked open the bathroom door.

"Ready for a cold one?"

"Sounds good."

He entered and handed me one of the tall dark bottles of imported beer, put down the toilet lid, and sat beside me, companionably sipping from his.

"I save the imported for special occasions."

"If this doesn't qualify, I'll replenish your supply."

I closed my eyes when I finished the bottle and lay back to relax.

"Sit up and I'll dry your hair." His voice was husky.

I straightened and he began toweling my hair. Eventually I reached down and released the drain switch and stood. He wrapped me in a large bath towel, picked me up and maneuvered us out of the bathroom without cracking a knee or elbow, and headed across the hall.

"My gown," I protested.

"You put it on and I take it off. What's the future in that? Do you still want pizza?"

I didn't answer and he decided that meant no. We ate cold pizza at three A.M. and went back to bed.

19
"The Day After"
August 28, Wednesday, 8:00 A.M.

Hank was gone when I awoke. I stretched and assessed my physical condition. Some residual soreness lingered in my muscles. The soles of my feet were tender, but with the proper pads I should have no difficulty walking. After stumbling around in the darkness of the swamp for hours, I felt surprisingly well. I smiled and wondered how much Hank's visit last night contributed to my well-being.

I jumped up and hit the shower to keep from thinking about all the problems our renewed relationship could bring. I fed Bobby Lee and Rudy and myself, and had just poured my third cup of coffee when Jasmine walked in.

"How did the search go?" I asked as she headed toward the coffeepot.

"Four hand-rolled joints and two rocks of crack tied in a handkerchief. I'm terrified of that conveyor maw at the lumber mill. Have you been there when they're feeding whole *trees* into those blades?"

"Yes, I have. I had a nightmare about three years ago, when I first started searching there. I could see a dog, excited over smelling drugs, breaking free and getting hung up by its leash and being pulled into those jaws, with me still hanging on. We give the machinery a wide berth now, but why take chances? Let's cut out searching that area entirely. Tell the foreman our insurance forbids us to go within fifty feet of those blades. If the men are stupid enough to use drugs and run that saw at the same time, they should be the only ones at risk."

"Thank you! I find myself gripping the lead so hard my fingers cramp."

"No more."

She smiled. "Changing the subject . . . how did it go last night?"

"Don't tell me you didn't peek to see if Hank's unit was parked by my back door early this morning?"

"I fell asleep in the tub last night, I was so tired. If he stayed, he was gone before my alarm went off this morning at five."

I gave her a smug grin. "The cold pizza was superb."

She laughed. "I'm so happy for you both!"

"Whoa, this is not a match made in heaven. I'm just cautiously optimistic."

"As you should be," she agreed. "Have you called Susan yet?"

"Oh Lord, I haven't. She'll skin me alive if she isn't the first to know. I've got to call her right now."

"I'm training in the north field for the next two hours if you need me." She rinsed out her coffee cup and waved as she left. I punched in Susan's number.

"Browse and Bargains, Susan speaking."

"Good morning, how goes the day?"

"Great, so far. And how's yours?"

"I slept in this morning. Had a search and rescue last night I wanted to tell you about—"

"Let me interrupt. I got up very early this morning, did ten laps around the cinder track at the high school, and had a disgustingly cholesterol-loaded fattening breakfast at Sam's Place with our favorite sheriff."

"Hank?" I said, surprised.

"Duh, how many favorite sheriffs do we have in common?"

I bit my lip. "What did he tell you?"

"All about your successful rescue, getting dunked, your blisters, et cetera, et cetera. I didn't want you to think that I didn't have all the facts. This way, you don't have to tell me all the details. How are the blisters?"

"Not bad." I was about to rain on her parade. She thought she had all the facts? "Guess who stayed over last night."

She took a quick indrawn breath. "What's his name? Baldy?"

"Who?" God, I was acting thick-headed and half asleep. She meant Leland Kirkland, Leon's elder brother, who I had bragged about meeting Monday morning. "No, no. To tell you the truth, he had slipped from my thoughts completely."

A short silence. "Surely you can't mean that convict Jimmy Joe? Are you out of your mind?"

I let out a weak giggle. "I see I have to give you a teensy-weensy hint. Hank."

"Hank? Really?"

"Cross my heart."

"He didn't say a word! We were together for over an hour this morning and he failed to mention a peep about it."

"What can I say? He was being a gentleman. You remember the last time we broke up and how upset I was when he assumed too much, too soon? I guess this time he decided to let me do the announcing."

"I don't want you to take this wrong, but it seems very sudden. Several days ago, you were ready to boil him in oil. You two have a history of off again and on again. You know I love Hank and wish you both the best, but come on, Sidden, are you sure this is gonna work?"

"How can I be sure? I can't issue an ironclad guarantee."

Hadn't I already heard the same doubts earlier from Jasmine? I was beginning to feel like the little boy who cried wolf once too often.

"Of course you can't. I was being silly," she said quickly. "But be careful!"

The installer for the security gates arrived with a helper just before three and finished shortly after five. Wayne and Donnie Ray had removed the gates from the storage barn and had them leaning against their respective posts. The underground wiring was still there, sealed in conduit. It was a simple matter to install the new alarms and hook them up.

Sneaky Pete kept giving me furtive glances, and when he presented me with the worksheet to sign, he blocked his helper's view with his wide backside as he clumsily pocketed his early-bird bribe with a conspiratorial wink. I felt like washing my hands, but I gave him a curt nod and chalked it up to doing business.

I now had my electrified fence and early-warning systems on my two gates. Anything or anyone weighing thirty pounds or more who entered would set off a raucous noise that would alert us to intruders. Wayne's alarm also had lights that would flash in his bedroom, living room, outside his front door, and throughout the kennel. After almost a year of freedom, we were now back to living under siege conditions. I just prayed that Jimmy Joe would slip up and either be captured or lose his fascination with the bloodhounds and me.

I wondered if I would have to reconsider my vow that I wouldn't be the one to go after him. I still thought that he had gotten a raw deal with the ridiculous sentencing, but mainly he had forged his own fate and I wasn't responsible for his incarceration.

I needed a plan. After ten years of passive defense of my life and property with Bubba, I didn't feel like going through it again with Jimmy Joe. I spent a few minutes wallowing in self-pity. Why me? How could I be the object of harassment and stalking for the second time in my life?

After ruminating awhile, I decided on a course of action. I needed to know more about Jimmy Joe's relatives in this area. Maybe I could get someone who cared about him to pass on a message from me. I would let him know again that I commiserated with his misfortune and would assure him that I would not mount a search or be party to trying to capture him and return him to prison. For these promises I expected him to forget any feelings he claimed to hold for me and to leave me to live in peace. Sounded good to me; it was worth a shot.

For supper Jasmine and I dined in style, with candles, cloth napkins, and tablecloth on the kitchen table. We had thawed an already cooked small roast with potatoes, carrots, and Vidalia onions, a contribution from Rosie, Wayne's mother, who worried that we would eat only junk food if she didn't keep the freezer stocked with real home-cooked meals. The four of us within the compound contributed money each month for the groceries and everyone was pleased with the arrangement. Rosie knew we had nourishing meals and we didn't have to slave in the kitchen. Jasmine tossed a salad and I made drop biscuits from Bisquick. Wayne and Donnie Ray had left early to attend the stock-car races in Waycross.

I pushed my plate away with a groan. "I ate too much, as usual."

"I'm surprised that you haven't gained back the twenty pounds you lost during the trial. You haven't, have you?"

"Nope, I'm still at one hundred and eight pounds. Isn't it wonderful? During the past twelve years, I have gone on crazy diets to lose two pounds and would gain three right back. How is it possible?"

Jasmine seemed lost in thought. "Well . . . you're getting older. Maybe your metabolism has finally stabilized."

"Older?" I said huffily. "You're just jealous because I weigh less than you and eat what I want."

"You got that right," she agreed, eyeing my slim figure. "Enjoy it while you can. The process could reverse itself any day now."

I just grinned at her. I momentarily ached for a cigarette at least a foot long. The craving still haunted me sometimes after a full meal, a chocolate bar, or my first cup of coffee in the morning. I pushed the thought away and began to idly fold and unfold my dinner napkin.

"Hank didn't call me today." I tried to sound casual.

"Did he say he would?"

"No. But he always called a lot . . . before."

"Maybe he was really busy today."

"Maybe," I said slowly.

"Did you call him?"

"Call him? Why should I call him? It's his place to call me!"

"Says who?"

"He always did before," I said with asperity.

"Well, it always failed before. Maybe he's trying to conform to new standards, maybe he thought you didn't like him calling you so often."

"He should call me."

"Jo Beth, if you want to speak to him and hear his voice, call him. It's as simple as can be."

"He should call me," I repeated.

"Fine."

She began to clear the table and I got up to help. After the dishes were washed, she said she had to study and left early.

I decided to call Little Bemis. He was my contact, the one who did all my computer searches and raided large institutions for pertinent information. Due to being a computer nerd and quitting the high school football team after only one season, he had had a very difficult time in school, as the whole county was counting on him to be the great white hope for winning the state championship. Now he works for a large corporation and has a responsible job, but suffers from one grand illusion—that he is the last great spy in the universe. I feel silly when I have to look up the code of the day before I call him for information using my code name, and couch my requests in mythical fantasy, but I'm not silly enough to make an error. One deviation from the set protocol and he would hang up; I would never be able to use his valuable services again. I dialed his home number, and when he answered I began my weird request.

"Chief, this is Lila of Lilliput. I heard about some humbugs today?" This took care of my code name and the day's code, which was *humbugs*. "The name for the case file is 'The Pale Prince of Prison.' The subject is Jimmy Joe Lane. I need every relative you can find, however tenuous the connection, his or her current address, phone number, employment, and if any one of them owns property."

"Anything else?"

"No, sir."

"Use drop nine by ten hundred hours tomorrow."

He hung up before I could say thank you.

"Toto, we're not in Kansas anymore, that's for sure," I said into the silent phone before I replaced the receiver. I picked up the list of twenty different drops and groaned. Number nine was under the train trestle at Jackson's crossing, almost in the center of town. How could I explain crawling under there if anyone spotted me?

I sighed and eyed the silent phone. Picking it up, I

dialed Hank's home number. It was still early, just after nine.

"Hello."

The female voice that answered had a soft drawl and a dulcet tone. I was so shocked I couldn't make my voice work.

"Anyone there?" She now sounded amused. "Hello?"

"I'm sorry . . . I dialed the wrong number," I said with precise diction when I finally got my tongue unglued from the roof of my mouth.

"No problem," she answered.

Hank has two sisters, three sisters-in-law, and bushels of female cousins that live in this town, but I was certain none of them would answer his phone sounding as if molten honey was dripping from her jaws. Suddenly I was standing in a desolate landscape without a stitch of clothing on and feeling the cold wind chill my bones. I went to bed to get warm.

20
"A Week After"
September 4, Wednesday, 8:00 A.M.

I smiled at Miz Jansee across the steam table as I headed for the wall phone. The buffet was loaded with everything that constituted a great Southern breakfast: sausage, bacon, ham, grits, red-eye gravy, scrambled and fried eggs, sausage gravy, buttermilk biscuits, home fries, and pancakes. She had been cooking since six.

The common room was bright and cheerful. The tablecloths were soft pink with dark wine-colored napkins. Lena Mae, the maid, had cut pink- and wine-colored rosebuds, white baby's breath, and a sprig of verdant fern for the cut-glass bud vases on each table.

I picked up the chirping instrument. "Hello."

"How's everyone doing?" Susan asked.

"Great. You sound chipper this morning."

Susan always enjoyed the week-long seminars that we hosted once a month to introduce law-enforcement personnel to our bloodhounds and to train them in how to live and work with the dogs in the future. It gave her a chance to meet six different males and to practice her feminine wiles. I had detailed dossiers on all six, so she knew who was single and who was married and out of bounds. She faithfully came for cocktails and supper each evening and stayed for the conversation afterward. Each night she was dazzling in her different and startling choices of garments. Jasmine and I were awed as much as the men.

"Have you heard from you-know-who?"

She was referring to Hank.

"Not a peep or a visit. It's as if he has disappeared from the face of the earth."

"When are you gonna call him?"

"Have you heard me mentioning hell freezing over?"

"Don't you want to hear what he has to say?"

"Not particularly. Silence is very telling."

"Well, I'll see you a little after six."

"Looking forward to it," I told her truthfully, ending our conversation.

Someone had activated the jukebox and country ballads were playing softly, creating a soothing background sound to the clink of silverware and coffee cups, and the murmur of conversation. I was feeling fine. The seminar was going well, no major glitches so far, as I mentally knocked on wood, and I wasn't a mental case from Hank's inexplicable behavior, as of yet. Congratulating myself for my sensible attitude, I took a deep breath and felt pangs of remorse and abandonment slice into my rib cage and careen into my gut. I diagnosed them as acid from stress and detoured to the kitchen to take some fizzy stuff.

Back at the table, the plate I had loaded down with enough food for a starving family of four, before the phone call, now looked grotesque. I caught Jasmine, at the next table, looking at me with a questioning expression and I gave her a weak smile, a short negative shake of the head, and then picked up my fork. I would eat if it killed me.

"Isn't that so, Miz Jo Beth?"

The young woman speaking was a trainer, Nola Faye Dowling, who had just turned twenty-one. She was a pear-shaped dishwater blonde who wore Coke-bottle glasses, and had no discernable breasts and wide hips. She also had a smart mouth and an abrasive personality—which is why I placed her at my table so I could watch her like a hawk—and I had no idea what she had just said.

"I'm sorry, I didn't hear you."

She tossed her head with impatience and nodded abruptly toward the man seated to her right.

"I was telling Sergeant McHenry that Matilda is slow,

and that he shouldn't coddle her and hold back when she hesitates. He has to be firm with her."

I gave Nola Faye a benign smile although all I really wanted to do was march her behind the barn, out of sight, and shake her till she rattled.

"I'm acquainted with your speech patterns, Nola Faye, but you don't want to confuse Sergeant McHenry with your choice of verbs."

I turned to him to continue.

"Nola Faye meant that Matilda is slow in movement, not in brains and knowledge. I would describe her as thoughtful and thorough. What I've noticed the past two days is the fact that you two seem to work so well together. I believe that we achieved a fortuitous match when we paired you with her, sight unseen."

He beamed from my praise, and my accompanying smile included Nola Faye, but she didn't see it. She was looking at her plate. She knew that she had yanked my chain and that I was furious with her. Little Miss Troublemaker had achieved another tiny victory in that I was forced to notice her and to correct her nonsense. I wished that I didn't understand her insecurities so well. I'd then have been able to cheerfully fire her soon after she was hired.

When I saw that most had finished eating, and Lena Mae was picking up empty plates and refilling coffee cups, I rapped on my water glass and got everyone's attention.

"Welcome to day three of your training session. It seems that you are all bonding nicely with your animal partners. As I told you at the first breakfast meeting, if anyone has any doubts about the bloodhound we have chosen for you, any personal dislike of our choice of the dog we paired with you, please feel free to speak to Jasmine or me and we'll try to remedy the problem.

"Wayne will now show you what we will be doing this morning. We come back in from the field at eleven-thirty, lunch is at twelve, and we resume training at one-thirty."

Wayne, who was seated at the head of the third table, stood and slowly turned so that the sixteen of us could easily read the printed message on his Etch A Sketch: "One-on-one man trailing on a mile-long course."

Chairs were pushed back and people began heading for the kennel to pick up their dog and take him or her to the training field to the right of the building. Some detoured to the rear of the room where the rest rooms were located. I sat and finished my cup of coffee.

I told myself I should remain here and help Wayne, Jasmine, and Donnie Ray, but I had called Jimmy Joe's parents last night and had a ten o'clock appointment to see them this morning. Little Bemis had come through with some very complete records; I had the family listed through the past three generations. It was amazing in this day and time that so many of them had remained here and hadn't moved on. Jimmy Joe was obviously not the only one in this family who loved swamp life.

My large pegboard in the office had red and blue pushpins lining the edge of the swamp in this and two other adjoining counties. Red was for family members' home sites and blue was for their property. When I was working on the large detailed county map and placing the pins, I felt envy that Jimmy Joe had so many living family members. I had no doubt that each and every one of them was intensely loyal to him and would help him if he asked. I felt as if I would be taking on an army of enemies if I changed my mind and decided to seek him out.

I had one blood cousin who had skipped the country when his plan for my incarceration had failed. I had some third cousins who lived far away who were on my adoptive parents' family tree and who wouldn't put me out if I were on fire, and that was it in my family.

I didn't miss having relatives until I saw others, like Hank and Jimmy Joe, who had so many. I only missed what I didn't have when I was blue and I had been in that state since Hank had taken me to bed and then disappeared into the woodwork the following day. Our sleeping together was as much my idea as his. I had reached for him willingly and eagerly. After seven days, I had to face the fact that his abandonment was deliberate and cruel. Mea culpa. My former behavior of quickly kissing him off was the reason I was now in pain. Obviously, he was getting even, or giving me tit for tat, or whatever.

I spoke with Lena Mae and repeated her duties for the rest of her shift. Repetition was not wasted time in regard to Lena Mae. She was slow moving, tightly packed in her tall frame, a farmer's daughter who hummed country tunes as she moved languidly through her eight-hour shift. When I had first hired her, I tried to tutor her, to improve her reading skills and interest her in thinking about her future. She had been polite, inattentive, and simply not interested. After six months I admitted defeat. She was content with her life and had no future expectations.

I met Donnie Ray going out the door. He was loaded down with his camera, extra lens, and a portable light reflector. He puts together a video of the six men who attend each of our seminars, with candid sequences of them working with their dogs, and ends it with them posing with their canine partners at the graduation party, the men dressed in their department's full uniform. We mail them a copy as a souvenir of their visit.

"How's it going?" I inquired.

"The shots from yesterday turned out fine," he said with little enthusiasm. He didn't look happy.

"And . . . ?" I knew something was bugging him.

"It's Wayne. He's acting funny, you know?"

"I'll talk to him as soon as I get a chance. We've all been busy the past few days. Got any ideas?"

"He hasn't talked to Amy lately and she hasn't been by. Last night I asked him if they had a fight and he like to have bit my head off. You think they've broken up?"

"Give him some slack until I can find out what's going on, okay?"

He shrugged and brushed by me without answering.

I checked the kennel but I was sure that Wayne was already out in the field where they were holding the man-trailing exercises. I went to the north door of the common room and gazed out at the stick figures several hundred yards away milling around with dogs in tow and decided to wait until this afternoon.

I went to the house and debated with myself whether

or not I should change clothes. The only occasions that we dressed up for around here were church and funerals. I decided my jeans and T-shirt would put Jimmy Joe's parents more at ease.

I ran a brush through my hair and put my wallet in my hip pocket. Bobby Lee took off for his leads, hanging on the back porch, and Rudy stretched, then came out to watch. He knew he was not welcome in the common room while meals were being served. He was banned because he circled each table, abandoning all dignity and begging piteously for food. He didn't enjoy riding in the van or the car. He only tagged along to see if Bobby Lee was going or staying.

I slipped on a pair of gloves as Bobby Lee stood on his hind legs and gently unhooked both leads from the large nails in the post rail. He pranced back to me trailing leads and drooling slobber. I kept the six-foot lead and carefully placed the twenty-foot lead, where the hook protruded the correct distance, back in his mouth and told him to hang it up. He raced back and worked it over the nail after several tries.

I knuckled Rudy's chin and told him to guard the fort, then Bobby Lee did his jiggle dance all the way to the garage. I had grown so protective of him that it was influencing my decisions about using him for dangerous searches. He couldn't understand why I seldom took him with me and why he was banished to languish on the porch, awaiting my return. I loved all the bloodhounds in the kennel, but Bobby Lee was special. He owned my heart and we were soul mates. I couldn't force myself to put him in a dangerous situation, which meant I wasn't using the best talent that would ever be available in this kennel.

Today I was going for an interview with Jimmy Joe's parents and would take Bobby Lee along to enjoy the ride.

21
"You Can't Choose Your Relatives . . ."
September 4, Wednesday, 9:00 A.M.

Bobby Lee sat in the passenger seat next to me in my truck, alert to every sight passing by us. He really did need to get out more, I thought, with a pang of guilt over how protectively I'd been treating him. But I couldn't deal with it if ill came to Bobby Lee because of wrong choices I might make.

Wrong choices . . . like the choice I'd made to welcome Hank back into my bed—and my heart?

I pulled over into a Quik-Mart parking lot and sat for a moment, hands braced on the steering wheel. Where the hell had all this emotion come from? Just this morning, I'd been competently—more than competently—overseeing breakfast of day three of another training seminar. Now, unforeseen, unbidden, and unlikely emotions were welling up in me.

What I needed, I told myself, was to clear up the clutter in my life. That included forgetting Hank on a personal level, once and for all, although I knew I'd still have to work with him professionally. That also included making sure Jimmy Joe Lane didn't intrude any longer on my hard-won freedom—the task at hand with this morning's visit to his parents. Then I could focus on my work. That would be enough to see me through this life, right?

"Right?" I said aloud, looking at Bobby Lee. He looked back at me and drooled. I grabbed a cloth from under the front seat, mopped up the drool, and made a decision. I needed a cup of coffee and another look at the map to figure out how to get to Jimmy Joe's parents' house. It wasn't as though they lived in a neat, trim little house in town that had a mailbox bedecked with large neon numbers. The senior Lanes—Obediah and Netty—lived farther out from Balsa City than Beulah and Hiram Burton, off one of the dirt roads on the edge of the Okefenokee swamp.

I tried to remember which red pushpin signified their home on the map of Lane family members I'd created on my office pegboard. The fact that when I'd talked to Obediah the night before his directions had included a "then turn left at the big rock and you'll see our place" didn't inspire much confidence. I pinched the bridge of my nose between my thumb and forefinger. I needed more caffeine to see this through.

I clipped Bobby Lee's lead on his collar and we went on into the Quik-Mart.

As I was pouring myself a cup of coffee that smelled burned, a woman, her hair piled high up on her head in a woolly-looking beehive, and wearing a blue-and-green-plaid cotton dress and yellow house slippers, came over to me. She peered at me with cloudy, gray eyes, and said, "No animals in the store."

I ignored the comment, and walked over to the

counter. There she was again, behind the cash register, peering at me with those eyes. "No animals in the store," she said again.

"This," I said, "is a highly intelligent, talented bloodhound."

"Still an animal."

I lifted an eyebrow. "You want me to just leave now or should I stay long enough to pay for the coffee?"

She took my money. I put the change in a collection can for the Humane Society. "A donation," I said, "from my bloodhound." I made sure to emphasize that last word. Cloudy-eyed Woman said nothing.

Back in the truck, Bobby Lee settled down in the passenger seat while I sipped my coffee—which tasted a lot better than it had any right to, given its burned smell—and stared at my county map and the instructions I'd written out for myself the night before. When I got my bearings, I pulled out of the Quik-Mart and headed toward the Okefenokee.

The Lanes' house looked much like I expected it to, modest, grayish-brown clapboard, single story. A screened porch ran the length of the house and was filled with rockers. I understood that. The Lanes had no air-conditioning, most likely, which would drive people out onto the porch to try to cool off, or at least to seek relief from the stifling inside heat. The screening would be necessary to protect porch sitters from dive-bombing bugs.

Towering moss-laced cypress trees overshadowed the cabin and other trees, oak, mostly. I never fail to be impressed by cypress trees.

There were more than a dozen trucks and cars—all older—filling the front yard. No other junk, though. If Jimmy Joe ever needed to make a clean getaway from here, he'd have plenty of options to choose from, assuming he knew which options ran and which were just for parts. Scruffy grass grew tall around the tires of about half of the vehicles.

So why, since the Lane homestead fit the image I held of it in my mind, did something strike me as . . . off? The house, yard, trees, cars shimmered in the mid-morning heat. Even though it was early September, this was still going to be a hot day.

Too hot, even at ten in the morning, to sit in my truck.

I clipped the lead onto Bobby Lee's collar and we got out of the truck and headed up to the house.

I hollered out a "hello" at the porch steps, and when there was no answer, let myself and Bobby Lee in through the screen door. I knocked on the wood door to the house. Again, no answer.

I checked my watch—I was on time. I frowned. Obediah Lane had been excited the night before to hear from me, more than eager to welcome my visit. He'd even called out messages to his wife, Netty, as we'd talked: "It's that Jo Beth Sidden woman, Netty. Says she wants to come and visit a spell."

I was muttering under my breath, about to knock again, when the door jerked open. Standing in the door frame was a large man, and the sight of him made me inhale sharply. I'd expected a potbellied good-old-boy in a T-shirt, overalls, and working boots, with a craggy face and two days' worth of beard scruff.

I'd gotten the good old boy part right—there's something unmistakable, and undisguisable, about the type—and the craggy face. This man was a bigger, beefier version of Jimmy Joe, a vision of what poor Jimmy Joe might have looked like had he not existed all this time on prison fare. None of this was surprising.

The pin-striped navy suit, white dress shirt, and red tie certainly were. As was the cleanly shaved face, dotted here and there with toilet-paper spots where an unpracticed hand had brought the razor too close to skin. Did I mention we only dress up for church or funerals? Unless Obediah had a midweek service to attend, or someone in the Lane clan had just passed away, I couldn't understand why he was so dressed up. Suddenly, my T-shirt and jeans seemed inadequate.

Obediah peered at me for a long moment. I was just about to explain who I was when he suddenly broke into a wide, toothy grin and pulled me to him in a viselike hug that clamped my arms to my sides, squeezed all of the air out of my lungs, and pulled my feet up off the porch floor. I couldn't even find my voice to protest.

"Netty Netty, come quick! She's here! She's finally here!" Obediah hollered. The scent of Obediah's breath was an odd mixture of moonshine and mint mouthwash.

"Well, lawd, Obediah, put the poor girl down afore you squeeze the livin' daylights out of her." I couldn't see the source of the tinny, chirping voice because Obediah's hug had pressed my face into his chest.

But Obediah obeyed the voice, setting me down carefully, then stepping back. I caught my breath and a view of the source of my rescuer's voice at the same time.

Netty was as tiny and slender as Obediah was tall and beefy. She looked more like a doll-woman, although her thin face was well striped with wrinkles. She had on a fifties-style belted, navy blue dress that was crisp yet shiny from repeated ironings. That Obediah and Netty had mated to create Jimmy Joe seemed humorous, in a surreal sort of way.

Netty also had her hands on her hips, a dust cloth in one hand, a stern expression on her face as she gazed at Obediah, who was looking sheepish. Now that I could breathe again, I saw that she was clearly in charge, and I saw the humor in that as well. I suppressed a smile while thinking, Good for you, Netty.

Netty gave me a sweet smile. "Now you come on in, sugar pie, and make yourself at home." She suddenly remembered the dust cloth in her hand, stared at it for a moment in horror, then tucked it behind her back while waving me on in with her free hand. That's when it hit me—she and Obediah had dressed up, and cleaned up their house, solely on account of my visit. I felt my heart drop into my solar plexus. Surreal—and scary—was only beginning to describe the scenario that I'd created by my phone call the previous night, and into which I was now walking.

I stepped into the neat, wood-paneled front room, which smelled heavily of pine-scented cleanser. The overstuffed couch and two side chairs were covered in faded rose chenille that was now patchy with threadbare spots, many of which had been covered by crocheted doilies in a rainbow of colors—purple, white, blue, red, green, yellow, pink, and even brown—giving the furniture a bizarrely polka-dotted appearance. There was one coffee table of rough-cut pine, one end table with a lamp. No rugs, no books, no magazines or newspapers, no knickknacks, no decorations beyond the doilies.

A wood-paneled wall, punctuated by a shut door, formed the back of the room and divided off the rest of the house, which I guessed would be a kitchen, two bed-rooms, and, I hoped for the Lanes's sake, a bathroom. The back wall was covered with newspaper clippings that had been cut out and tacked up. None of them were framed—just tacked up with a single tack at the top. As a result, they were all yellowing. And, I guessed, they were all about Jimmy Joe.

I wanted to go over and look at them, but decorum—and Netty's voice chirpily urging me to "take the good seat"—kept me from it.

By "good seat," I reckoned she meant the chair with the least number of doily polka dots, so I sat down in that chair. The Lanes sat down on the couch across from me, and beamed their wide grins at me, so I guessed my chair choice had been correct.

I cleared my throat, about to launch into my reason for being here, a plea for their help in getting Jimmy Joe to understand that he and I did not have a romantic rela-tionship—in fact, we didn't have any relationship at all—and that he needed to stay off my property and away from me entirely. But before I could speak, Obe-diah started talking.

"Just look at her, Netty," he said, beaming at me. "Prettier even than Jimmy Joe said."

Netty looked at me appraisingly. "She's fine. Good

bone structure. I expect their younguns will get Jimmy Joe's cheekbones, though. Seems to run in the Lane family, no matter what the womenfolk bring to the party." She laughed, blushing suddenly at her own reference to the concept of Jimmy Joe and me mating and creating future little Lanes.

"And that hound of hers," Obediah said. "You can see it's fond of her. Just like Jimmy Joe said." Then his face collapsed into a frown of worry as he looked at Netty. "You think it's right, though, a woman bonding with a dog like that? I mean, training bloodhounds might be fine for a man—"

Netty gave him a reassuring pat on the arm. "Don't you worry, now, Obediah. Once she's settled down with Jimmy Joe, she'll want to give all that up, like a good and proper wife."

Netty looked at me then. "Course, now, it's going to be hard for Jimmy Joe to settle down, him on the lam from the law. So you can stay here with us. Or in our special hideout—"

"Shh, Netty. You know Jimmy Joe don't want us telling her about that till after the wedding." Obediah looked at me and beamed, all his worry about my "unnatural" bonding with Bobby Lee apparently forgotten for the moment. "Did you know there's a song about Jimmy Joe? We thought it would be nice to have that sung at you-all's wedding—after 'Amazing Grace' of course."

"We hope you don't mind us picking out the music, but we want to go all out. It'll have to be a secret swamp wedding, what with Jimmy Joe on the lam again," Netty said. "We've got the date set for next month, the twelfth—Jimmy Joe's birthday! Did you know he picked that date and planned his escape just to have your wedding on his birthday? Isn't that sweet? Maybe there'll be another verse or two added to his song, about your wedding, then you can be in the song too."

"Jimmy Joe said you'd be the best birthday present ever," Obediah added, with a wink, chortling until Netty elbowed him, at which point he winced and started to redden. Netty took his renewed silence as an opportunity to start rattling on again, this time about possibly letting out her wedding dress for me to borrow, and all the foods the clan would bring in for the post-wedding feast—which would have to be held in a secret location, of course—and her one cousin who played good banjo music and her other cousin who played harmonica, so we could also have a dance, and so on, and so on.

Looking back, it would probably have been easier—and saved a whole lot of trouble—if I'd just seen the absurdity of the whole situation and excused myself from the Lanes's house, laughed all the way back to town, then sworn out restraining orders on the whole clan.

But I didn't want to have to do that. It brought back too many memories of being pursued by my maniac ex-husband, Bubba. And I didn't want to swear out a restraining order as that would have meant calling Hank, who I'd decided I'd never voluntarily talk to again. And I surely didn't see the humor in being discussed as if I were some fantasy come to life—a female commodity—for Jimmy Joe Lane.

"Mrs. Lane," I said, startling her a little with my interruption. "You'll need to contact your cousins and cancel the wedding music—"

"You have someone else you want to do the music?" Netty said, looking alarmed. "Oh, Billy and Jeb will be so disappointed—"

"Please! Listen to me!" I ground the next words out between my teeth. "Listen carefully. I. Am. Not. Marrying. Your. Son. Not next month. Not ever. Do you understand?"

Obediah and Netty stared at me, eyes wide with shock. Clearly, they didn't understand—at least not fully. I sighed, went on with what I hoped would be an explanation that would clear everything up. "Look, I don't know quite why Jimmy Joe has this fascination with me. But it has got to stop, okay? I'm not in love with Jimmy Joe. I never even met him until a few weeks ago. I am not marrying him. In fact, I came here because I hoped you'd get him to understand he has to get over this obsession with me. He must leave me alone."

They continued to stare.

"Now, look," I said. "I refused to do a search for Jimmy Joe after he escaped from Monroe Prison. I figure that means you owe me one. Please, save us all a lot of heartache and get it through to Jimmy Joe that he needs to forget about me and leave me alone."

Obediah started shaking, looking for all the world like a little boy who's just been told that no, he's not going to get a coveted toy after all. "But—but—he told us about all the letters you and him sent to each other. Poems. Love poems. How your tender words got him through all those awful nights in the prison, giving him the courage to break out again and again . . ."

I swear, the man actually sniffled and wiped a tear from his eye.

"Mr. Lane, I don't know what all Jimmy Joe told you, but I've never corresponded a single word with Jimmy Joe. Your son is living in a fantasy world and the best thing you can do for him—"

"Are you calling my boy a liar?"

I turned my attention to the woman who a moment ago was swooning over the chance to become my mother-in-law. Now, she stared at me with hard, glittering eyes. Under different circumstances, this was a woman I could admire for her sheer grit.

She stood up, hands on hips. "No one calls my boy a liar," she proclaimed, spittle flying from the corner of her mouth. "You—you—hussy. You—you—whore of Babylon!" Her bird's chirp voice turned into a shriek. "You get yourself and that slobbering hound from hell out of my house, now! You'll pay for this—"

"Mrs. Lane, I came out here to reason with you—"

Obediah put his face in his hands and started crying. Netty put her fingers to her ears and squeezed her eyes shut in a hear-no-evil, see-no-evil pose. "Jezebel! Man hater!"

I didn't want to see what would happen if Netty Lane ran out of names to call me and decided to find a rifle and come after me.

I stood up, walked out, with Bobby Lee following me, and went back to my truck. Running would have been a more proper response, but I didn't want to give the Lanes the satisfaction.

When I got back to paved road, though, I broke the speed limit by more than a few miles per hour.

22
". . . But at Least You Can Choose Your Friends"
September 4, Wednesday, 10:30 A.M.

By the time Bobby Lee and I got back home, I was not only shaking all over, my stomach was roiling, my head was starting to ache, and I had an urgent need to pee. Too much weirdness. Too much caffeine.

I let Bobby Lee out of the truck—and let him take care of his call of nature first—before going into my house. Somehow, the fact that I'd needed to use the security code to once again get through my front gate to my property—shades of Bubba past—hadn't made me feel any better about my disastrous encounter with Jimmy Joe Lane's mama and daddy.

I got Bobby Lee settled inside, took care of my own call of nature, then swallowed some aspirin for my impending headache and some fizzy stuff for my stomachache. I lay down on my bed for a few moments, knowing that rest would give me a chance to recover and the medicine a chance to work, but as I drifted off, visions—of Bubba, of Jimmy Joe, of Obediah, of Netty—danced in my head in maniacally gleeful whirling rounds to banjo and harmonica music.

I jerked awake. I was too restless simply to lie still while awake. There was plenty of work that needed doing for my business.

I splashed some water on my face and ran a brush

through my hair. I left my room and headed to my office, but then a sly thought popped into my head. Maybe what I needed was some comfort food. A left-over biscuit—or two—with butter and honey. Surely I'd burned enough calories through Lane-induced anxiety to justify the snack?

Before I even got to the dining room, I heard clear peals of laughter. Male laughter, female laughter, twining together in a delighted chorus. I stepped into my dining room, and saw Susan and Lee Kirkland sitting across from each other, each with a cup of coffee, laughing and chatting as if this were *their* dining room, one they shared cozily on a regular basis.

I cleared my throat, and they both looked up at me with sudden guilty expressions, as if they'd been caught in some naughty act.

I went over to the table and sat down next to Susan, across from Lee. "Good morning," I said simply.

Susan glanced nervously at Lee—this man who previously she'd called "Baldy" when I'd referred to him as good looking—with an expression verifying that his hairline was no longer what interested her about him. "Uh, hi, Jo Beth," she said. "I just came by to chat with you about something—"

"—and she ran into me," Lee said. He smiled, apologetically. "We introduced ourselves and then I'm afraid I just started talking her ear off and then one thing led to another—"

"—and here we are, drinking your coffee left over from the morning's breakfast for the trainers, Jo Beth!" Susan gave a most girlish laugh.

177

Good Lord, I thought. They couldn't have been talking for much more than an hour and already they were finishing each other's sentences? This too was bizarre, but in a much nicer way than the visit with the Lanes had been.

I waved a hand, as if to brush aside their concerns. "Plenty of coffee here," I said. "You're welcome to it. Although I'm sure it's not my coffee that brought either of you here?"

Susan stared down into her cup. "I—I needed to talk with you about something, but I'm sure it can wait."

"Oh, please don't let me prevent you from—" Lee started.

"No, your need to talk with Jo Beth is more pressing," Susan said. "And really, I need to get back over to the Browse and Bargain." She looked at Lee, making her eyes wide. "That's my store," she added. "It's in the middle of town. You can't miss it. I'm open all day."

She started to stand and Lee stood up quickly, dashing around to our side of the table to carefully pull Susan's chair out for her. Good Lord, I thought again. A Southern man . . . with honest-to-God Southern manners.

Lee watched Susan go. I had a feeling that when he finished whatever business he had here with me, he'd find himself with a sudden need to go book shopping. I pushed back a smile at that. Good for Susan. Yes, I'd found Lee attractive. But I surely wasn't going to begrudge the fact that Susan and Lee obviously found each other much more than attractive—compelling was more like it. Anything to make Susan see the light about awful, womanizing Brian Colby. And Lee had suffered the tragic loss of his brother and sister-in-law. They could both use a dose of happiness.

Lee sat back down across from me. "I came by to let you know that things have finally worked out with Sherlock," he said. "Both my parents and Sara's parents have agreed to give up their ridiculous fighting over who gets custody of him. Taking care of a dog is too much for all of them. But they want him to stay in the family. Sherlock is as close to a grandkid as either side has." He paused, and gave a sweet-sad smile. "So Uncle Lee here gets custody of him."

"Oh, Lee, I'm so glad to hear that!" It was a relief to know that the pain the families of Leon and Sara had already experienced would not be extended through a fight over a bloodhound that should be cherished and loved. "How's it going with you and Sherlock?"

"Well, that's why I'm here. We're doing pretty well. But we could both use a little training," Lee said. "Actually, I need the training. I'm quite certain Sherlock is doing everything he should. But I've never been a dog owner. I find myself to now be a dog lover, but clueless as an owner. Since you and your people know Sherlock better than anyone else, I was hoping I could get a little training? Of course, I'm willing to pay whatever fee you normally charge—"

I waved my hand at him. "Never mind the fee. Consider the training a gift in celebration of your new addition to your family."

Lee started to argue, then stopped, thinking better of it. I like that—someone who knows how to accept a gift graciously instead of arguing about it. He gave that sweet-sad smile again. I wondered how long before his smile would be real and full. Maybe Sherlock would help with that. And Susan too?

"Thank you," Lee said.

"Where's Sherlock now?" I asked.

"In the kennel," he said.

"Come on. Let's get started." He stood up, started gathering up the coffee cups and saucers. "Don't worry about that," I said. "I'll make sure it's cleaned up later. I'm eager to get you and Sherlock started with one of our trainers."

When we got out to the kennel, I found Nola Faye Dowling—the young trainer who'd tried to give me and one of the officers a hard time at breakfast—and informed her that she could spare some time away from the officers' training to give one-on-one attention to Lee and Sherlock. She started to argue with me, then shut up when I pulled her aside and told her that her future depended on Lee's, and Sherlock's, satisfaction and success with her training. By the time I left Lee and Sherlock with her, she had forgotten about me and was focused on the task at hand.

Then I went to the common area, looking for Donnie Ray. I wanted to see if he had any more insight into Wayne's unhappiness. I couldn't afford to have Wayne be perpetually miserable, and since my attempt to straighten things out with the Lanes had failed, I was determined to wrap up at least one loose end today. Somehow or other, I wanted to get my life back on an even keel. Sooner or later, I'm hoping I learn that that doesn't mean solving others' problems.

Jasmine cornered me before I could find Donnie Ray, though.

"How did your interview with the Lanes go?" she wanted to know.

I gave a snort. "I'm now officially number one on the Lane family's most-wanted list, a fact that automatically makes me an endangered species."

"You're kidding, right?"

"Don't I wish. Seems they were in the midst of planning a large secret swamp wedding for Jimmy Joe and me next month on the twelfth, Jimmy Joe's birthday."

I saw from her bright eyes and amused expression that she wasn't taking this seriously.

"But you don't even know the guy. How did his parents get such a crazy idea?"

"Jimmy Joe has been feeding them bulletins of his undying love for me for more than a year now. His latest escape was planned to consummate the match made in heaven." I shuddered involuntarily at the thought. "And his parents believe every word he utters."

"This is ridiculous. They got angry when you set them straight?"

I thought about Obediah's sobbing and Netty's vehement howling of nasty names at me. "Angry doesn't accurately describe their feelings. I want you to know that my snotty attitude didn't land me in this latest mess. I am completely blameless."

"I believe you," she said with wide-eyed innocence.

"Watch it. I have a short fuse this morning . . . and I detect barely controlled amusement in your eyes."

"How's this—I believe you. I really, really believe you."

I sighed. "Keep practicing. Maybe you'll improve your act with repetition."

Jasmine made the wise decision to scoot out of my path.

Fortunately for her, I saw Wayne, consulting a clipboard as he moved slowly through the common area.

I went over to him, touched him on the arm. "How's it going?" I signed.

Wayne tucked the clipboard under his arm. "Fine," he signed back. "These officers are among the best students we've had, and—"

"That's not what I meant. I know the training is going well. If it weren't, I'd be in the thick of it putting it right. What I mean is, Wayne, how's it going with you?"

"Fine."

"What a lie."

He turned to walk away, but I put my hand on his arm. He stopped, but didn't turn back to me, so I walked around to face him.

"Wayne, what's going on with you?"

He looked up at me and his eyes were filled with so much anger and hurt that I inhaled sharply.

He tossed the clipboard to the floor. "Donnie Ray been complaining?"

"No, of course not! Look, Wayne, everyone can see that you're not yourself."

"Well, you're certainly being yourself, pushing for information that's none of your business."

I was shocked, not at Wayne's slam about my pushiness—because I knew that was true—but at his vehemence. This wasn't at all like Wayne.

I signed, "Fine, Wayne. You don't have to talk with me if you don't want to. But leave the crappy attitude behind when you're at work, okay?"

I turned to head back to my office, but apparently I'd awakened an anger in Wayne that wouldn't easily be put to rest, because he grabbed my arm. I turned to face him. He signed, his hand movements fast and angry. "You want to know what's wrong with me, Jo Beth? I'll tell you what's wrong. What's wrong with men like me is women like you!"

"I think you'd better explain yourself. I'm giving you three sentences to clarify that statement."

He grinned—and his grin was an uncharacteristically nasty mock smile. "One—what's wrong with men like me is women like you and Amy. Two—you say you want decent, kind, loving, basically good guys, but then you say we're not exciting enough, it'll never work out, whatever. Three—then you take off and either find yourselves lonely or hooked up with someone no good because you're just too damned scared of a real relationship that might be nice and kind and lasting even if it's not perfect or exciting all the time and you wonder why—poor, poor, pitiful you—you're so miserable."

I stared at him, stunned. "Okay. Apparently you and Amy have broken up and you're unhappy. Fine. How does that lump me in with Amy?" I was sincerely confused. Wayne, as far as I knew, had not only been happy in my employ, but had also found my expectations, though high, to be more than fair.

Wayne sighed. "Boss, at the risk of hacking you off and finding myself unemployed, sometimes you can be pretty damn dense. Why am I lumping you in with Amy? Why don't you think about what I just said—then go ask Hank."

Wayne stopped, and caught his breath, as if he realized belatedly that he'd just gone too far. And he had.

"You will turn around and go back to work now. And you will never again discuss Hank with me or any of my relationships, for that matter."

For a moment, Wayne looked at me, blinking hard. I realized he was fighting back tears. Then he turned and walked away.

I made it back to my office. I sank down into my chair, telling myself I had work to do and that I needed to come up with a clever way to get Jimmy Joe Lane— and his family—to leave me alone once and for all. Plenty to do, plenty to do . . .

And yet I found myself with my head down on my desk.

What if Wayne was right?

I thought, uncomfortably, of Susan and her unsatisfactory relationships with men like Brian Colby and now her apparent attraction to Lee. Were Susan, Amy, and I really all of a kind, subconsciously sabotaging good, yet imperfect, relationships and exchanging them for those that promised excitement but could never possibly bring anything but pain?

I tried to clear my head of such ridiculous doubts, but then, unbidden, Hiram and Beulah came to mind. Was their secret simply that they'd stuck together, even when things were tough, because they really cared for each other as individuals? How else to explain the way Hiram looked after Beulah even now when she was only a fragment of the woman he'd married?

And on the other end of the spectrum were Leon and Sara. One had apparently betrayed through infidelity, and the other had murdered.

Where did I fit on that spectrum?

Sometimes the universe delivers answers to such soul-searching questions.

Sometimes the universe just delivers up a wicked sense of irony.

I got the latter.

My phone rang.

I answered.

And on the other end of the line was Hank's voice, saying, "Jo Beth, we have a call out. Beulah has gotten herself lost again in the Okefenokee."

23
"Once More . . . with Feeling"
September 4, Wednesday, 11:00 A.M.

My conversation with Hank was crisply professional and to the point. Beulah Burton had again slipped from the house. Hiram had slept late and just woken up around ten-fifteen A.M. He'd searched the house and immediate grounds for her several times before calling Hank, in a panic. Please, Hiram had begged Hank, help me find her one more time . . . and then for her own safety as well as Hiram's peace of mind, he'd do what he realized he should have done long before, and find a nearby nursing facility for Beulah.

I said that of course I'd do the search. Hank stated that he would be by my compound shortly so that we could caravan over to the Burton place. I started to argue that that really wasn't necessary—I remembered the way to the Burton place and could easily find it again on my own, thank you. But I didn't trust my voice, given my emotional state at the time of Hank's call, and so I said that would be fine.

Focusing on an urgent task helped snap me out of my earlier wallowing in self-pity and soul searching. Of course Hank was an idiot. And so was Wayne. Hiram, I told myself, was the last remaining decent guy living on the face of the earth. In fact, he was probably the only decent guy who'd ever lived on the face of the earth— a guy created by God in Her infinite wisdom to serve as an example to all the other men about how they should be, but weren't. So of course I'd find Beulah for Hiram. Hah.

I was trying to decide which bloodhound to take this time—probably Gulliver, since he'd done the earlier search—when there was a tap at my door.

"Open," I said.

Jasmine stepped in.

"I was just going to come for you," I said. "We have a call out. Believe it or not, poor Beulah Burton has wandered off again, and—"

I stopped. Jasmine looked distraught. "What's the matter?" I asked her.

"Mama. My mama. She's had a bad diabetic reaction.

I just heard about it from someone at church. She went to the hospital last night." Jasmine sank down into one of my visitors' chairs and put her face in her hands. "Oh, Jo Beth. I didn't even know she was diabetic."

Relationships. It wasn't just the ones between men and women that were thorny.

I sighed. "Jasmine, I'm sorry to hear this. I'm sure she'll be all right, though, and——"

Jasmine looked up, wiping away tears. "I know, that's what I keep telling myself. But this is the last straw. I'm going over to her house right now."

"I thought you said she was at the hospital."

"She is. But she's supposed to be coming home sometime today, then have in-home nursing care. I've decided, Jo Beth, that I just have to sit myself down in front of her house until she'll at least talk to me. I'm sorry. I don't know how long it will take, but I've got to do this."

She looked at me then, awaiting a response.

Jasmine hadn't even heard me say we had a call out, I realized.

I looked at her, considering all she'd been through in her life, and all she'd done for me. This was clearly important to her.

"Of course you have to do this," I said. "Go. Take all the time you need. This training session is going the smoothest of any we've ever had, so we'll be fine."

And, I told myself, I knew the territory around the Burton property pretty well by now. My suspicion too was that for whatever reason, Beulah had taken off again for the river. Maybe, in what was left of her reasoning, it represented something of great importance. In any case, Gulliver and I could do the search by our-selves.

"Thank you, Jo Beth. You don't know what this means to me. Someday, I'll find a way to repay you, and—"

I waved a hand at Jasmine, signaling that she should stop talking. "I have one condition for letting you off—with pay, of course—on this mission of yours."

Jasmine lifted her eyebrows at that. "Yes?"

"Don't get hurt," I said, emphasizing each word care-fully. Jasmine knew I wasn't referring to physical injury. "If you realize there's no point in continuing your vigil, do yourself a favor. Give it up. And come home."

Jasmine looked at me for a long moment, weighing, I knew, the implications of my "condition." Perhaps her mama, given her brush with serious illness and possibly death, would finally soften and give Jasmine a chance to talk to her. Or perhaps her mama had become so hardhearted that she'd want nothing to do with Jasmine, even in these circumstances. The latter possibility would be hard for Jasmine to accept, I knew. But she needed to, for the sake of her own mental health.

Finally, Jasmine nodded, her face composed in a grim expression. "I understand what you're saying." She stood and went to the door, opened it, started to leave, then stopped. She looked over her shoulder at me. "Thanks."

I felt a crack in my heart from the gratitude—and fear—that Jasmine managed to convey in the delivery of that single word.

I waited a few moments after Jasmine left. Then I stood up, and headed for the kennel. Jasmine had to do what she had to do. And now I had to do likewise. Duty—and a meeting with Hank—called.

Five minutes later, I was in the kennel, snapping the lead on Gulliver's collar and talking quietly with him about our pending assignment.

"What the hell do you think you're doing?"

I froze at the sound of the voice—Hank's voice. The sudden tight feeling in my chest was not the reaction I'd anticipated. I was going to be cool, right? Because I didn't care about Hank anymore. . . .

Hank's angry words and tone of voice were also not what I'd anticipated. He was supposed to be conciliatory and groveling, humble and begging my forgiveness.

Reality somehow never jives with my expectations of it.

I stood up, looked at Hank, felt anger at the unbidden thought of my God, he really is as sexy as I thought, and the anger came out in my words. "I know what I'm doing," I said, emphasizing the "know" coldly. "I'm getting Gulliver ready for our call out to search for Miz Beulah." I gave him a small, cool smile. "Or were you just making that up to come over here and apologize?"

I regretted the words the minute I spoke them.

"And what the hell would I have to apologize for?" Hank asked, with a mixture of amusement and anger that infuriated me further, and destroyed any chance at all that I could act cool or detached.

"If you don't know, maybe the little floozie who was at your house when I called a week ago can explain it to you," I said.

I moved away from him, toward the door. Gulliver and I had an elderly lady to find. To hell with Hank.

But Hank was not one to be walked away from easily. He put a hand on my arm, stopping me. I jerked away, ready to warn him to never use physical means to control me. True, his touch had been light, a brush of his hand against my arm, really—but suddenly I was in fighting mode. Any excuse to have it out with Hank would do.

He spoke before I could, though, his amusement quickly gaining on his anger. "That floozie you refer to happens to be Marietta Mae Jones, a second cousin twice removed on my mama's side. I haven't seen her in twenty years. But she thought she'd stop by on her way from Florida to Ohio and say howdy."

I glared at Hank. "We're not exactly a direct stop on the interstate between Florida and Ohio. Am I really supposed to believe she just wanted to say hi to her distant cousin?"

Now Hank gave me a full-fledged grin. "Nope. She wanted to say hi, spend the night, and borrow a few hundred bucks." He shrugged. "I gave it to her."

"Lovely. I'm so glad you're so damned generous with your kin. I'd like to get over to the Burton place now—"

"Why didn't you just tell her who you were?"

"Why haven't you called?" It was the question I'd promised myself I'd never ask, but there it was. And I wanted to know—much, much more than I was willing to admit.

Hank sighed. "Because I knew that sooner or later, something like this would happen, Jo Beth. You not trusting me. You doubting me." He paused, sighed again, then gently traced a finger along my cheek. "You finding a reason to break us apart, because I know you, Jo Beth. You're afraid of real relationships." He shook his head. "The night we were together was so . . . good. I don't think I can handle having that ripped away from me again and again."

His words were so much like Wayne's that I flinched. But before I could react—and I wasn't sure if I wanted to defend myself or castigate Hank for not at least talking with me about this issue—he abruptly changed the subject.

He pointed down to Gulliver. "What the hell do you think you're doing?" It was the question that he'd opened with.

"I'm getting a well-trained bloodhound prepped to go on a search," I said matter-of-factly.

"Why *this* bloodhound?"

"Gulliver do something to offend you?"

"Oh, come on, Jo Beth. You know what I'm getting at. Are you ever going to take Bobby Lee out on a search so he can exercise his God-given talents? Or are you just going to keep hiding and protecting him too?"

Well, Hank hadn't lived the days and nights of fear and nightmares that I had because of Bubba. Who the hell was he to judge my management of anything?

"Go to hell, Hank," I said quietly. "No one tells me what to do with my bloodhounds, least of all with Bobby Lee."

I stalked from the kennel, but Hank's words sailed after me. "What you're doing is wrong, Jo Beth. And you know it. Hide yourself from a real life if you want. But you don't have any right to hide Bobby Lee from the life he was meant to live."

If Bobby Lee hadn't been on the porch of my house, staring across the field at Gulliver and me as we emerged from the kennel, I don't know how things would have turned out later. Maybe we—Hank, Bobby Lee, and me—were all destined to go through the hell we experienced over the next weeks sooner or later. Maybe not taking Bobby Lee that day would only have postponed what was meant to be. Or maybe not taking Bobby Lee that day would have meant that our lives would have taken a turn down a different path—one that, in the end, would be safer, but not the right path for any of us.

In any case, Bobby Lee was on my porch, and he was staring at Gulliver and me. And it seemed to me that through that unspoken bond that can develop between a human and an animal, Bobby Lee was asking me, "Why? What have I done?"

So I turned, and reentered the kennel, glaring at Hank as I started to unleash Gulliver.

"Fine," I said. "You're right about one thing. Bobby Lee hasn't been on a search in far too long and I'm taking him on this one. But, Hank, don't you ever try to tell me my business. And get the hell off my property. I don't need to follow you to get to the Burtons' place, or anywhere else, for that matter."

24
"Hide and Seek"
September 4, Wednesday, Noon

Hank, wordlessly, did get the hell off my property. Ten minutes later, I was in my truck, Bobby Lee by my side.

I grinned, knowing how excited Bobby Lee would be to work a trail again. But I was also shaking—and hot. Maybe the shakes were because of my encounter with Hank. Or maybe from nervousness over taking Bobby Lee out again. Or maybe just a combination of all that, plus the encounter with the Lanes, with Wayne, and even my conversation with Jasmine about her never-ending quest for recognition from her mama.

Whatever had me stirred up, when I saw the Quik-Mart I'd stopped at earlier, just ahead, I made a quick decision to pull in and treat myself to something cold and soothing. A lemon-lime Frostee might not solve my problems, but it would sure soothe them. Comfort food. Second time that day. But then, thanks to Susan and Lee, I'd never gotten to the biscuits and honey. And, I told myself, I sure didn't want to get dehydrated during this search. Sure, I had water bottles. But lemon-lime Frostees . . . Oh, yes, they were well known to help prevent dehydration. At least, that's the little white lie I told myself as I pulled into the parking lot.

"Quick stop at the Quik-Mart," I told Bobby Lee.

The same dour woman was on duty. I plunked some change into the Humane Society can before she could say anything. "Another donation from my well-trained bloodhound," I said with a grin.

Then Bobby Lee and I went over to the self-serve Frostee machine. I had just put the lid on my drink and was unwrapping the straw when the woman came up behind me.

"You Jo Beth Sidden?"

I finished putting in the straw, carefully folded the straw's paper wrapper—taking my time about it—then deposited the wrapper in the trash bin. I turned around, looked at the woman, took a long sip of my Frostee. Ahhh. Refreshing coolness and tartness, all in one. A drink I could relate to.

"Who wants to know?" I asked, finally.

"Someone on the pay phone by the front door for you."

She walked away, toward the cash register at the counter.

I frowned. Who would call me here? Who could possibly know about my unplanned stop? But maybe Hank had backtracked to tell me the search was off, Beulah was found, and he'd called me from his unit. It was the only explanation that made sense.

I paid the woman, who took my money wordlessly while avoiding eye contact. I put the change, again, into the Humane Society canister, and put my Frostee on the edge of the check-out counter.

Then I turned to the pay phone, picked up the receiver, and said, "Hank?"

There was, for a moment, just heavy breathing on the

other end. Finally, then, a voice spoke softly. Insidiously.

"That hurts me, Jo Beth, it really does, to hear another man's name come from your lips."

Oh my God. It was Jimmy Joe Lane. How had he found me here?

"My parents told me about your visit and how poorly it went," he said. "I don't cotton to folks hurting my mama and daddy, not even you, Jo Beth. They were right disappointed in your lack of appreciation of their plans for us."

"Now, you listen to me, Jimmy Joe, there are going to be no plans for us—"

"They're going to keep an eye on you, Jo Beth. And if I don't like what I hear, I may just have to have a little encounter with Bobby Lee. Just to get my point across to you. Which would make me right sad, because really, I do like Bobby Lee, and he seems to like me, and I think the three of us—"

"Don't you dare threaten Bobby Lee," I said, grinding the words out through my teeth. "Don't you dare—"

But then the line went dead.

I slammed down the receiver, whirled around, wanting to ask the clerk who worked here what Jimmy Joe had said to her—but the woman was gone. And I was late for my appointment to find Beulah. I grabbed my lemon-lime Frostee and headed out the door with Bobby Lee.

We got in the truck and took off. I was shaking now, even worse than before. I grabbed the Frostee, took another long drink, but somehow, now, it didn't seem so satisfying . . . or comforting.

I was sweating profusely by the time I pulled into the Burtons' lane.

Pull it together, I told myself as I got out of the car. I was not only sweating, I was shaking and dizzy. Maybe the call from Jimmy Joe had just been too much to add on top of an already difficult day, I told myself.

Tracer, I thought vaguely, as I let Bobby Lee out of the truck. I should have a tracer done on the phone call, find out where Jimmy Joe had been calling from. He was an escapee, a wanted man. And he'd threatened Bobby Lee. He'd threatened Bobby Lee. . . .

"Jo Beth! Are you okay?"

I looked up at Hank—at two Hanks, actually. I must have been coming down with something. Hank was swimming before my eyes. I was dizzy. I was sweating. And my stomach was starting to hurt.

"I'm fine, of course I'm fine."

Was I hearing things too? My normally crisp tone had become almost slushy.

"Jo Beth, you don't look so good," Hank said, taking me gently by my arm. "You're unsteady. If you're not up to the search, you should say so. It's not a crime. We'll find someone else—"

"There is no one else!" I snapped. That wasn't entirely true, of course. We could get Jasmine to do the search. I knew she'd break off her vigil at her mama's house to help me if I asked. But I was in a prideful mood. "You wanted me to do the search with Bobby Lee, and now we're here. We're gonna do the search."

We argued a bit back and forth then, Hank and I—at

least, I think we did. It's hard to remember all the details, even now. I must have been my usual stubborn self, though, because my next clear memory is of being in the woods with Bobby Lee.

I was so hot that I had trouble breathing. In fact, I was panting hard, following along behind my prize bloodhound. The overgrown path looked familiar—yes, this was the path that had led us to Miz Beulah on our last search.

And Bobby Lee was in his glory—excited, nose to the ground, checking to the left and the right, clearly following Beulah's scent . . .

. . . yet, I didn't remember giving Bobby Lee Beulah's scent from her clothing or other personal item. But I must have, right?

My stomach lurched and I realized I was in danger of throwing up. I was miserably hot, feverish. Tired. Too tired . . .

I pulled up on Bobby Lee's lead. He stopped, looked back at me.

"Sorry," I mumbled. "Sorry. I'm just so tired . . . hot. . . ."

At least, that's what I recall mumbling as I sank to the ground.

Bobby Lee came over, whining, licking my face. I looked into his warm eyes, focused on them. Those big, soulful eyes of his. He was a searcher, I thought, and I was too. But what was I searching for? What?

I shook my head. I knew I needed to try to think clearly. I was sick. Maybe the flu?

But no. I'd had no symptoms until just a bit ago. And

I'd had none of the warning chills that precede getting the flu.

Food poisoning, then. I tried to think. I'd had breakfast, of course. But if breakfast was the cause, my symptoms should have kicked in a lot earlier.

That extra biscuit with honey. But no, I hadn't actually gotten around to my biscuit-and-honey snack. I tried to remember. No, I'd had no biscuit, or anything else . . .

Except the lemon-lime Frostee.

I stared into Bobby Lee's eyes, our noses touching, his breath warm on my face. I knew I had to hang on to him then—because I suddenly knew we were in danger. Very, very deep danger. I couldn't even feel the lead in my hand. I couldn't even raise my other hand to touch Bobby Lee. I should try to get the walkie-talkie, tell Hank I needed help, but I couldn't move.

I could only stare into Bobby Lee's eyes, fight to stay conscious, while a distant, tiny portion of my brain realized the awful truth—I'd been poisoned at the Quik-Mart. While I was on the phone with Jimmy Joe, listening to his threats against Bobby Lee, someone had put something in my Frostee. The woman who worked there. Had to be her. No one else had been in there. But why?

Somehow, the woman must be connected with Jimmy Joe, and he was the one who'd put her up to poisoning me. . . .

No thoughts came after that realization.

Just the vision of Bobby Lee's eyes, staring into mine. And then . . . fade to black.

25

"Where, Oh Where Has Bobby Lee Gone?"
September 4, Wednesday, 1:20 P.M.

The first time I came to, I was alone.

Alone.

No Bobby Lee.

For a few minutes, stomach pain and sickness pulled my concentration away. I vomited until I had the dry heaves, leaving my body feeling as wrung out as an overused dishrag. My mouth was filled with a metallic taste.

But even more horrifying, I was alone.

"Bobby Lee," I hollered—or tried to holler. In my head, I was screaming. But my voice came out as a weak, cracking whimper.

"Bobby Lee! Bobby Lee! Bobby Lee!"

I was close to hysteria. Some part of my brain began barking sharp commands.

Check watch!

It was just twenty minutes after one P.M.

Oh God. I'd been out for an hour. Long enough for Bobby Lee to have gone far away.

But Bobby Lee wouldn't have left my side. Not voluntarily.

"Bobby Lee! Bobby Lee! Bobby Lee!"

Stop! commanded the tiny drill-sergeant part of my brain, which was struggling to retain control of my thoughts and actions.

I stopped—and realized with surprise that somehow,

I'd gotten to my knees and was crawling down the path.

Get the walkie-talkie! my inner drill sergeant ordered. I felt for it on my person, but it wasn't there. Hadn't I clipped it to my belt, as usual? But it wasn't there.

I backed up the few feet I'd managed to crawl and saw that the walkie-talkie was nowhere near where I'd been. I felt for it under the brush on either side of the path, and came up with nothing more than dirt and foliage. The walkie-talkie hadn't fallen off me. It had been taken.

But then something else, farther back up the path, caught my eye. I crawled to it, and stared in horror. Bobby Lee's lead and collar were coiled in a neat pile just off the path. A grubby piece of paper was pinned to the collar.

I picked up the collar and, with trembling hands, unfolded the note. Written in a penciled scrawl, with the sophistication and spelling of a second-grader, was a message that wrenched my heart:

Jo Beth,

I'm sorry it's come to this, but I figure it's the only way to get your attention. Come to me and I won't hurt Bobby Lee. But jest you has to track me. If you send anyone else, I can't account for what might happen to your bloodhound. By the time you find me I know you'll have time to think it thru and see we're ment to be together. Forever.

JB + JJ.
Jimmy Joe.

I had to find Bobby Lee—even if it killed me. Bobby

Lee was a bloodhound to die for.

And maybe, once I got my hands on Jimmy Joe, to kill for.

"Bobby Lee! Bobby Lee! Bobby Lee!"

Clutching his collar and lead so hard they cut into the palms of my hands, I got on my knees. I couldn't get up any farther. But I walked on my knees up the path, repeatedly bleating his name, not caring a whit that my knees were being torn up on the rough path, or that again my stomach felt as though it was being sent through a shredder.

When I came to the second time, my vision was filled with whiteness. In the background, I could hear hushed sounds, low voices talking. Something like shoes tapping on a linoleum floor, then the sound fading quickly.

My whole body, particularly my stomach, felt sore. My head throbbed. Something was poking into the inside of my left wrist.

I tried to lift my right hand and was surprised that I could. Carefully, I patted the inside of my left wrist and felt a thin tube and bandaging. An IV. I was in the hospital.

I blinked at the whiteness, then stared at it, until finally I realized that I was simply looking at a curtain that had been pulled around my bed.

Bobby Lee.

I had to get out of here, find him. . . .

I tried to sit up. My stomach muscles spasmed painfully and I fell back on the bed.

I must have moaned, because abruptly the voices

stopped. The curtain jerked open, and suddenly Hank was beside me, hovering over me, his hands curling gently over my left hand.

I pressed my eyes shut and felt wetness seep out from under my lids and down my cheek.

Bobby Lee.

This time, his name must have come out as a whisper, because I heard Hank say, "We'll find him. Right now you just have to focus on getting better."

"No." I'd found my voice at last, but it was raspy and shaky. "Bobby Lee—Jimmy Joe took him—there was a note . . ."

"I know," Hank said softly, patting my hand. "After a while, when I couldn't get you on the walkie-talkie, I got worried. We sent out a search party and found you fairly quickly. Bobby Lee's collar and lead and the note have all been collected as evidence."

"I have to search for Jimmy Joe . . . it's the only way . . ."

"Jo Beth, you have to give yourself time to heal first."

"No! There is no time." I opened my eyes and looked up at Hank. "I must find Bobby Lee. Even if it kills me."

Hank frowned. "You're lucky to be alive, Jo Beth."

"My drink—I had a Frostee from the Quik-Mart—it was poisoned somehow—the woman there—"

"I know. We have her in custody. I'll tell you about it later."

I lifted my right hand, which still felt leaden and slow, and grabbed his arm. "Now. I want you to tell me now."

Hank started to argue, then stopped. He shook his head and gave a quick laugh. "I should have known.

Even on the edge of death, Jo Beth, you're as stubborn and demanding as hell."

"That shouldn't surprise you," I said. "Now, tell."

He sighed. "Fine. Here's the synopsis, but save your questions for later. After we found you, you were muttering about Bobby Lee and that you'd been poisoned with your drink. You were able to tell me you thought it was the woman at the Quik-Mart. The emergency crew got you here and the staff pumped your stomach—not that there was much to pump out."

"I don't remember that."

"Be glad," Hank said abruptly. "There was a little bit of liquid left in the bottom of your cup. It had been dosed, all right, with isopropyl alcohol. Better known as rubbing alcohol."

I moaned. "The woman at the Quik-Mart—"

"Believe me, I got her in for questioning. She's Mona Estelle Lane, Jo Beth."

Mona Estelle . . . the name rattled around in my head for a few minutes. It was familiar, but I couldn't place it immediately. Then I remembered. That was one of the names from Little Bemis's report. Mona Estelle was an unmarried cousin from Jimmy Joe's father's side.

"She doctored my drink while I was on the phone with Jimmy Joe. Did I tell you about that call?"

"No. You can tell me later—"

"Now. I'm telling you now." As best I could, I explained to Hank about the call from Jimmy Joe that I'd gotten while I was at the Quik-Mart the second time.

"Mona didn't tell me about that," Hank said, "but she did admit to putting the rubbing alcohol in your drink."

"Jimmy Joe must have put her up to it, but how did he know I was there? Did she call him?"

"She didn't say." Hank paused. "Jo Beth, I'm guessing that he has all kinds of kin keeping an eye on you."

I closed my eyes, trying to think, trying to put it all together. The Lanes—and friends who would help them—were numerous. Somehow, Jimmy Joe had learned about my call out to the Burtons' place. That wouldn't be hard—the Lanes lived close to the Burtons, at least close in Okefenokee swamp terms. Practically neighbors.

He'd probably planned on catching me while I was on the search for Beulah, but when I went into the Quik-Mart, I unwittingly gave him an even better chance. Mona Estelle would have given him a call while I was getting my Frostee. Jimmy Joe would have told her to doctor my drink with something that would make it easier to subdue me. And of course, among the tiny first aid and medicine section of the Quik-Mart would have been a few bottles of rubbing alcohol, commonly used to clean wounds.

But deadly if ingested. It would only take a little— maybe a teaspoon—to do serious damage. Between the fact that I had gulped my drink quickly and the fact that I had been extremely upset about Jimmy Joe calling me at the Quik-Mart, I easily missed any off taste in my drink.

And because I'd ingested it quickly, and on a fairly empty stomach since it had been hours since breakfast and I'd skipped lunch, the alcohol had worked quickly, giving me an extreme reaction. In essence, the rubbing alcohol had poisoned me, as if I'd consumed a large quantity of drinking alcohol quickly.

I started pulling at the IV in my arm. "I've got to get out of here, start a search for Bobby Lee."

Hank pulled my hand away, then held both my arms down against the bed.

"What are you doing?" I shrieked. "Didn't you hear me? I have to get out of here! I have to go find Bobby Lee!"

"Jo Beth, stop! Ripping the IV out of your arm isn't an option. It's a glucose solution that you need to counteract the effects of the poisoning. You need it for at least another hour, and then you need several hours of rest and observation before you're sent home. There's nothing you can do right now, and if you try, you could end up making yourself even sicker. We almost lost you, Jo Beth. And I know you don't want to die."

I tried to jerk away from Hank. I tried to sit up, but I was too weak. "I don't care if I die," I screamed. "I have to find Bobby Lee. Don't you get it?"

"Jo Beth, I do get it," Hank was saying quietly. "But you have to understand a few important things before you start ripping out your IV and running from the hospital. The only way you're going to get Bobby Lee back is to calm down and let logic prevail. That should tell you that, number one, you can't find Bobby Lee if you're too sick to move—and for the time being, you are. And number two, you'll remember that you can't search for Jimmy Joe and Bobby Lee—no one can—until we find someone who has an article of clothing or other personal item from Jimmy Joe that we can use to give his scent to another bloodhound so you can track him."

Hank's words sank in. He was right. And then the absolute horror of the situation hit me. All those Lane relatives who adored Jimmy Joe. Who among them would possibly agree to help me find him . . . and Bobby Lee?

When I started sobbing, Hank let go of my arms, and pulled me to him, holding me gently. For once, I didn't resist being comforted.

26
"A Little Help from My Friends"
September 4, Wednesday, 7:00 P.M.

At the sound of the knock on my bedroom door, I struggled to sit up a bit straighter—no easy feat considering that I had a breakfast tray over my lap and that I was still weak. I probably would be for several days.

I knew who was probably knocking at my bedroom door—Hank. He'd brought me home from the hospital, when the doctor finally said I was ready to be discharged, and insisted on staying to help me get cleaned up and settled in bed. Then he'd insisted on providing me with a bit of nourishment.

Now, even as I smoothed my hair back from my face, I told myself that, given our recent argument and Bobby Lee's abduction, I shouldn't give a damn about what Hank thought of my looks. But the truth was, I did.

I cleared my throat. "Come in," I said.

I sounded a bit stronger than I had in the hospital,

although not yet as strong as I would have liked.

The door creaked open and Hank walked in. He came over and sat on the edge of my bed and peered appraisingly at the contents of my tray.

"Hmm. I see you don't like my cooking. How did I manage to screw up applesauce, chicken broth, and dry toast?"

I'd nibbled on the toast, had a spoonful or two of the applesauce, and sipped at the broth—all of which had seemed like a Herculean effort given my lingering queasiness. At least I'd gotten a prescription-strength dose of Tylenol before being discharged from the hospital, so the heavy throb of a headache was now just a dull ache.

"It was all fine, Hank. I'm just not quite up to eating much yet."

Hank nodded, a suddenly serious and worried expression coming over his face. I gave him a light jab in the arm. "Hey, look at it this way," I said, trying to be lighthearted. "Being nearly poisoned to death is a great way to make sure I don't gain back weight."

"I've always thought your appearance was great, Jo Beth. You know I like how you look—and feel—just fine."

I turned away from him. I wasn't ready for this conversation.

"Last time we were in this room, we shared cold pizza and beer," I said, and immediately wanted to hit myself.

"And had a good time," Hank said, taking my hand. "Look at me."

I kept staring away.

"Jo Beth," he said quietly, his voice a command. I don't respond well to commands. But then he said my name again. "Jo Beth." This time it was a plea. I looked at him.

"We could have good times again. I want us to. And not just now and again. I want you to be my wife, Jo Beth."

I sucked my breath in, hard, at that.

He smiled. "I know Not the best-timed or most romantic proposal in the world, given the circumstances. But dammit, I almost lost you today. You know how loss feels, especially now with Bobby Lee gone."

Tears sprang into my eyes.

"I'm sorry," Hank said. "But take how you're feeling now. That's how I felt when I thought I'd lost you permanently. At least when we were apart and I knew you were alive and healthy, I could get mad at you and even hate you at times because the hope of getting back together was there, way at the back of my mind, so deep I didn't even know it. I almost lost that hope today because I almost lost you."

"Hank—I—"

"No, wait, I'm not done. I want you to know something Hiram said to me this morning about Beulah. He said that during their decades together, he and Beulah didn't always like each other. At times, they might even have doubted their love for each other. But they never lost sight of the fact that as a couple, each one of them was a better individual than they would be apart. I think that's us, Jo Beth. I can't guarantee that we'll always like each other or get along or not fight. But I think we're better individuals together than when we're apart." He gently touched my cheek. "So what do you say, Jo Beth. Marry me?"

I closed my eyes, let myself give in to the sensation of spinning. So much had happened—so much that I needed time to think about. But I didn't have much time. I had to find Bobby Lee—soon. And I had to give Hank an answer—an honest-to-God, final and true answer—soon.

I opened my eyes and looked at him. "Hank," I said. "If I answer now, I'll forever wonder—and so will you—if my answer was based on my emotion over losing Bobby Lee."

"I know," he whispered.

I put my hands to his cheeks, and tilted his head up. I smiled at him. "Your question deserves a truthful answer. I don't want to answer from weakness. I want to answer from strength. Help me find Bobby Lee. And once we've found him, ask me again." I took a deep breath. "And I will give you an answer that's honest and true. And final."

Hank took my hands from his cheeks, held them a long moment, and then kissed each and every fingertip—slowly, lingeringly. Ten tiny delicious kisses.

"I will, Jo Beth Sidden," he said. "I will help you find Bobby Lee. And then I will ask you one last time to marry me."

Hank stood up then and lifted the tray from my lap. "I'll get this cleaned up," he said, walking toward my bedroom door. "And then we'll get to work on figuring out a plan to find Bobby Lee."

"Hank?"

He stopped at the door and turned.

"What about Beulah?"

He smiled. "After you were settled in at the hospital and I knew you were going to live, I sent a team down to the spot where you and Jasmine found her the last time. Sure enough, there she was. She's okay, much to Hiram's relief, and he's making good on his word to find a suitable, and permanent, nursing home for her, where he can visit her every day. In the meantime, she's in the hospital."

He left then, and I stared at the door. I was, I realized, willing him to come back. Partly because he was so damned sexy and even now I wanted a follow-up to those ten tiny kisses. But mostly, there was his character. Despite all we'd been through—all I'd put him through—he was so sturdy, dependable, dedicated.

A memory echoed in my mind. Hadn't I thought those very words were perfect to describe Hiram the first time we'd had to search for Beulah? Hadn't I lamented that while I was sure God must still make such men, I was sorry that so many women just didn't know how to find one?

The telephone rang. I reached to answer it, then hesitated. The last time I'd answered a telephone had been at the Quik-Mart, and the call had been from Jimmy Joe and I'd been poisoned.

I couldn't start hiding from life now—I never had before. I picked up the telephone, answered with a sharp, "Hello."

"Oh, Jo Beth, thank God."

It was Jasmine. I smiled at the warm sound of her voice. "I guess you've heard what happens to me when I go off searching by myself."

There was a gasping sound on the other end, and I knew that Jasmine was crying. "Oh, Jasmine, I'm sorry," I said. "I didn't mean that to sound so awful. I was just trying to make a joke."

"I know, I know," said Jasmine. "Wayne came by and told me what happened. Thank God you're all right. But Bobby Lee—"

"I'll find him, Jasmine," I said. "If it's the last thing I do."

"I want to help. If I had been with you, if you hadn't been alone—"

"Don't do this to yourself."

"I'm coming home. I want to help."

"Are you still at your mother's?"

"Yes. I've set up camp with a lawn chair, a cell phone, an umbrella just in case, and a six-pack of diet soda."

Despite everything that had happened, I smiled at the image. "Has your mama spoken to you yet?"

A long silence, then a sigh. "Not yet."

"Then you stay there," I said firmly. "I'll make sure Wayne or Donnie Ray or Hank comes by to check on you every few hours, but you stay right there until you wear her down."

"But, Jo Beth, I want to help you—"

"The best thing you can do for me is to stay right there. You're on a quest you need to finish. I am too."

Another long silence. Then, a tiny "Thank you."

"Don't thank me. Just take good mental notes so we

can share all we've been through the next time we can get together for a girls' night."

We said our good-byes and hung up.

I had just closed my eyes when the phone rang again. Again, I hesitated. How long before I could hear the telephone ring and not wonder if the soft, insidious voice of Jimmy Joe Lane would be at the other end, begging me to come be his wife—or else?

I picked up the receiver.

"Jo Beth? Sorry if I caught you at a bad time, but I just had to tell you—well, Lee came by my store late this afternoon, and we got to talking, all about Sherlock and everything, and then we went out to dinner and just had the most marvelous time, I mean we really clicked, and guess what? As soon as Lee brought me home, he gave me the sweetest little good-night kiss on the cheek, and—Jo Beth?"

"Yes?" I said, smiling in spite of myself. Susan's excited rambling was proof that some things in my world hadn't been rocked. I also wondered where her newfound bliss with Lee would leave Brian Colby. In the dust, I hoped.

"You haven't interrupted me yet. Are you okay?"

The image of Bobby Lee came to mind. "Yes."

"You don't sound okay. Are you sure you're not mad about me and Lee, because I know at one time—"

"Susan, Bobby Lee's gone."

There was a silence at the other end, then Susan's voice, quivering. "Jo Beth, did I hear you right? You said Bobby Lee is—gone?"

I told her what had happened since I'd last seen her.

"I'm so sorry," Susan finally said, quietly. "I want to help. What can I do to help?"

"Why don't you start by telling me what you came over to tell me this morning?" I said.

Long pause. I could feel Susan tensing up on the other end. Finally she said, "I will, Jo Beth. But now is not the time."

For once, I didn't argue.

"Okay," I said. "How about this—check in on me every now and again. I think my trainers can wrap up this week's seminar without much needed from me. All my concentration is going to be on finding Bobby Lee. That means I'm going to probably let small but important things slip or not have time to take care of them. Can I count on you to occasionally run errands for me, that sort of thing?"

"Absolutely," Susan said, some of the bubbliness back in her voice. I realized, with a pang, that the sudden loss of Bobby Lee seemed to have opened up a part of me where I'd stored away an understanding of relationships. It was as if I'd learned the art through Bobby Lee, and just hadn't realized it or needed to tap into it until I lost him—and had to fight to get him back.

I finished the phone call with Susan, then leaned back to rest. I'd drifted off to a peaceful dream—me, edge of a field, watching Bobby Lee chase butterflies—when there came another knock at the door.

I startled awake, straightened up, and watched Hank, Donnie Ray, and Wayne all come plowing through my door, carrying the bulletin board from my office, the bulletin board with all of the pushpins that signified where each and every one of Jimmy Joe's relatives lived.

Hank grinned at me. "We decided to bring the battle planning to you."

"Operation Recover Bobby Lee," signed Wayne.

"You can count on us," said Donnie Ray.

And I knew I could.

27
"Operation Recover Bobby Lee: Rough Beginnings"
September 6, Friday, 1:00 P.M.

Less than forty-eight hours after I returned home from the hospital, I—with the help of Hank—had exhausted every possibility of getting a lead on Jimmy Joe's whereabouts and, therefore, on Bobby Lee.

Mona Estelle Lane, Jimmy Joe's cousin and Quik-Mart employee, was only too proud to admit to poisoning my drink on Jimmy Joe's suggestion. She proudly admitted, also, to calling him each time I'd been in the Quik-Mart. But even threats of prosecuting her to the full extent of the law for attempted murder wouldn't get her to tell Hank one more thing, even when her state-appointed attorney urged her to do so. Hints that the prosecution might be willing to accept a lesser plea if she'd cooperate in helping us find Jimmy Joe did no good.

Her exact words were, Hank told me, proclaimed with a self-satisfied grin: "Jo Beth Sidden can go to hell before I'd help her out. No one calls Jimmy Joe Lane a liar and gets away with it. He told me she'd been writing him all this time with promises of love, and I believe him. She's not good enough for him. Besides, escaping from prison is a Lane trait that doesn't necessarily run in just the menfolk. I'd like a song written about me too."

Not much of a career track at the Quik-Mart for Mona, apparently, and she had never married or had children. From her point of view, she wouldn't lose all that much by going to prison on Jimmy Joe's behalf, and if it made her a secondary Lane legend, so much the better.

Warden Sikes, from Monroe Prison, where Jimmy Joe had been incarcerated, wasn't much help either. The few personal items that Jimmy Joe had left behind had been washed, disinfected, and stored away pending his return. There was no way one of my bloodhounds could pick up a scent from any of those items in order to track Jimmy Joe.

"You didn't want to track him before, Ms. Sidden," Sikes said. "Too bad that now that you have a personal reason for wanting to do so, it looks nearly impossible that you'll be able to."

I hung up on him for that comment.

Next, Hank and I paid a visit to Jimmy Joe's parents. Netty started howling obscenities at me as soon as she saw me. When Obediah finally got her calmed down, he looked at Hank—refusing to look at me—and said, "Why would we help this woman? She's broken our boy's heart. Now, seeing as how you don't have no paperwork making it official to be here, I suggest you get off my property, Sheriff."

As we left, I stared back at the Lane property. There was something about it that struck me as just . . . off. And there was something in my heart, which raced at the thought that Bobby Lee and Jimmy Joe were nearby, even if there was no evidence of either of them in the tiny house or on the property immediately surrounding it. Once I did get an article of Jimmy Joe's to use to start my search, I'd start near this property, that much I knew.

But finding someone to help me wasn't going to be easy. In two days, I called or visited or both called and visited every single Lane resident on the list Little Bemis had provided for me. And every single one told me, in some form or another, to go to hell.

Jimmy Joe had a whole extended network of family that was proud of him for catapulting into local fame as a man on the run from the law. Somehow, even among the religious zealots of the group (and I ran into a few who told me that uppity women like me would burn in hell), his lawlessness and ability to thwart imprisonment conferred on all of them a sense of status and accomplishment. In a nutshell, thanks to Jimmy Joe, Lanes everywhere could say, "Ha!" and thumb their noses at those in town who had long seen them as backwoods swamp rats who couldn't do much more than breed.

I understood their feelings.

But I needed to get Bobby Lee back.

That's why, on a Friday afternoon, I was in my office, contemplating a detailed map of the area surrounding Netty and Obediah Lane's property. Normally about this time I'd start looking forward to our traditional girls' night, but on this Friday that wasn't even an option. Susan, who had been by or called many times in the past forty-eight hours, was out with Lee, and I was glad for her. Jasmine, whom I'd checked in with several times via Donnie Ray and Wayne, was still on her mama vigil.

And I had a search to plan. It didn't matter that I didn't have the item I needed from Jimmy Joe—yet.

Somehow, I'd get it, even if I had to break into the Lanes's house. All those newspaper clippings hanging on the wall told me that his parents had probably created a mini shrine to Jimmy Joe in the second bedroom. And I was pretty certain that Jimmy Joe wouldn't have neglected to visit his mama and daddy. I was giving the universe twenty-four more hours to deliver what I needed, and then I was going to become Jo Beth Sidden, burglar. I wasn't motivated as much by desperation as by cold, calculating necessity.

I had turned myself into a completely focused machine, with one goal, and one goal only: Find Bobby Lee. Wisely, no one had commented about my crisp attitude and commanding tone. The inner drill sergeant had become an exterior drill sergeant. Everyone understood that that was the only way I could keep myself together.

My office door swung open and Hank came in. I didn't look up as he sat down across from me. I kept staring at the map.

"I think you've got that map gridded to perfection by now," he said softly.

"Just about."

"Jo Beth, we have to talk."

I kept looking at the map.

217

"We have to talk about what we're going to do about Bobby Lee now that it's clear we're not going to get a personal item of Jimmy Joe's for our search."

I had my back-up plan, of course. But I wasn't about to tell Hank, although I was curious to know his.

I smiled at Hank.

"Somehow, I didn't think my statement would amuse you."

"I'm smiling at the fact that you were referring to 'our' search for Bobby Lee."

"We're in this together," Hank said.

I nodded. "I know. And I'm grateful. What do you suggest we do?"

He sighed. "I know you're not going to like this." He shook his head. "I don't much like it either. But, Jo Beth, I think we're just going to have to wait Jimmy Joe out. Sooner or later, he's going to get tired of waiting for you, and he'll either set Bobby Lee free or return him to you in the middle of the night."

"You mean—just do nothing."

"What option do we have?"

Suddenly, I was angry. "If you're going to say 'we' in reference to finding Bobby Lee, then you'd better get rid of such an apathetic attitude. I don't wait for what I want. I never have. And I want Bobby Lee back—now. Sooner than now. How do I know Jimmy Joe won't hurt him, or hasn't already hurt him? What if you're right and he does set Bobby Lee free—what if a gator gets to him before he can find his way home?"

Hank stood up, slammed his hands against my desk. "God, Jo Beth, you make it sound as though I don't care about Bobby Lee when you know damned well I do. Just what are we supposed to do now, though?"

"How about question everybody again. Force them to help us. Look under every rock and twig if we have to—"

Hank stood up, then stalked to my office door. "I need a break," he snapped. He meant, I knew, from me—not from the work.

I slumped back in my chair, closed my eyes, pinched the bridge of my nose between thumb and forefinger. And that, I thought, was how it would be if we got married. We'd work as a team, sure, but fighting whenever our strong wills clashed. Which would be often.

I opened my eyes and went back to staring at the map of the Lane property, contemplating how to best break in to their house in the next twenty-four hours.

The telephone rang. I grabbed it.

And there was that soft, insidious voice again.

But after a few seconds, it registered that it wasn't Jimmy Joe. This was a female. And in my shock at thinking it was Jimmy Joe, I'd missed what she was saying.

"Excuse me," I said. "Could you repeat that please?"

A long silence, then an even longer sigh. "Pay attention this time. My name is Mary Sloan. I'm Mona Estelle Lane's sister. And I think I have something you want. But you have to come by yourself to get it."

28
"Operation Recover Bobby Lee: The Setup"
September 6, Friday, 2:00 P.M.

Mary Sloan was Mona Estelle Lane's sister, a thirty-something, twice-divorced woman who, unlike all the other Lane relatives Little Bemis had tracked down for me, did not live out in the countryside near the Okefenokee. She lived in one of the tiny apartments in a small, brick twelve-unit building on the edge of Balsa City.

Little Bemis had, of course, identified her and how she fit into the Lane family. Even knowing she was Mona's sister, I'd called her some time in the past twenty-four hours, hoping that she might at least want to convince her sister to be cooperative so that Mona could plead to a lesser charge.

When I'd suggested that idea to Mary, she'd had just two words for me: "Screw you." Then she'd hung up on me. At least her dismissal of my plea and me had been succinct. Most of Jimmy Joe's other relatives had opted for much lengthier descriptions of why I was unworthy of their aid.

But now I found myself standing outside Mary's apartment building, staring at the depressing little structure, wondering what I'd possibly let myself in for. On the off chance that she really did have a scent item for me, I had the necessary oversize sealable plastic baggie to collect the item and protect it.

On the more likely chance that this was just a setup of

some kind, Jimmy Joe and a posse of Lanes ready, willing, and able to beat the crap out of me, I just had my wits. I hadn't told anyone where I was going—I'd just gotten in my truck and driven away from my compound as soon as I'd gotten off the telephone with Mary.

Yes, I knew this was risky—even stupid.

But Mary had made it clear that she wanted to see me alone. And I was willing to take the risks—any risks—required to find Bobby Lee.

I stepped into the building. The heavy door slammed shut behind me. Despite the fact that it was early afternoon, the entryway was dim. It had a faintly musty odor but was swept clean. There were three rows of metal mailboxes, four per row. Mary had told me that her apartment was number 9, on the third floor. I looked at mailbox 9. Unlike the others, it wasn't labeled with the owner's name. Perhaps the mailman had memorized the fact that all of Mary Sloan's mail went into box 9. Or perhaps Mary had sent me on a wild-goose chase.

I climbed one flight of stairs, to the second level, and had to stop and rest for a moment. Normally, climbing stairs wouldn't have tired me, but I was still weak from the poisoning.

I climbed the next flight, went to the door labeled with a single "9," and knocked.

No answer.

I knocked again.

I heard movement inside and waited, deciding to count to fifty before knocking again. I had gotten to thirty-seven when the door swung open.

My heart lurched. Facing me with an amused grin on

her face was a clone of Mona. There were a few fine-tuned differences, but that just made the nearly perfect resemblance eerier. Mary's features, though, were accentuated with subtly applied makeup. Same upswept grayish-brown hair, but captured in a smooth French twist instead of an untidy bun. Also wearing a dress, but Mary's was a flawlessly tailored black knit, accessorized with a single strand of pearls.

The woman grinned at my stunned expression. "I guess your research didn't turn up the fact that Mona and I are twins. Identical twins." She stepped back, pulling the door more widely open, giving me plenty of room to enter her apartment. "Come on in."

I went in, and engaged her in the usual Southern hospitality conversation. Why, yes, I'll have a seat. The offer of sweet tea is so kind of you, but I'm afraid I must pass. The traditional Southern response would be a delighted Why, thank you, I'd love a glass of sweet tea, exclaimed as if such an offer was so rare as to be a surprise. In this case, I was taking a decidedly non-Southern route by declining the offer. Given that her twin sister had poisoned me two days before, precaution trumped tradition.

When we were both settled—Mary on a couch, myself on a chair that was catty-corner to her—I took the chance to glance quickly around. The furniture was elegant, a beautiful mahogany that was upholstered in rose-patterned chintz. The walls were lined with bookshelves that were filled with books. On a coffee table of carved mahogany was a crystal vase filled with three long-stemmed pink roses—real ones. And to the right of the vase lay the latest issue of *Martha Stewart Living*. The magazine was open to an article on collecting pepper mills; several lines of the article had been highlighted by a yellow marker that lay in the center of the magazine.

Mary caught me looking around the room. "Not the taste or decor you'd expect from a Lane descendant?"

I looked at her. "To tell you the truth, no. But then, I didn't expect that any Lane would help me out. In fact, the last time we talked, you had only two words for me: 'Screw you.' So I'd like to get to the point. Why did you invite me here?"

Mary laughed. "I like a woman who gets to the point."

And I liked the fact that she'd called me on judging her—but I wasn't here to exchange compliments. I wanted to know if she had any way to help me find Bobby Lee. If not, I wasn't going to waste my time with her. I looked at her and mentally picked up my counting at thirty-eight, giving her to one hundred to start talking.

I'd barely broken forty when she sighed. "Go ahead and take a good look around," Mary said. "I guess you could say I'm the real rebel of the Lane family, never mind that the ballad was written about Jimmy Joe." She gave a low, bitter chuckle and looked into her glass of tea, swirling the drink around, staring in the glass as if it held answers to long-held questions. I realized that she wasn't drinking just sweet tea and I wondered how often she stared into a glass of bourbon with those questions.

"I left home when I was twenty by getting married to my first husband, a man considerably older than me, and moving to Baton Rouge. He had a job there in sales—pretty impressive position, as far as my family was concerned, and I should have just been happy with being married to someone who was successful. But I wanted to try my own wings. I started taking college courses as I could afford them and eventually broke up with my husband—he thought I was trying to outgrow my place as his stay-at-home helpmate. And, of course, I was."

I shifted restlessly. What did Mary's personal history have to do with my getting Bobby Lee back? Possibly nothing. Possibly everything. I knew, though, that if I interrupted I'd never find out.

Mary went on. "We got divorced, I got a little money and a waitressing job and managed to get by while I worked on my college degree in English. After graduation, I started teaching at a high school. That's where I met Matt Sloan. My second husband—and the real love of my life." She smiled sadly. "I surely loved that man. He was a teacher too. Math." She gave another chuckle. "People used to tease us that we were at opposite ends of the academic spectrum, so how could things work out between us? Matt had a joke, that opposite academic disciplines attract to make a whole new field of endeavor—chemistry." She sighed. "We had some good years, Matt and I."

She took a long drink, stared again into the glass. "Then things started falling apart. There were cutbacks at the school. First I lost my job. Then I got a call from Mona—our mama was sick and she needed me to come back and help take care of her. I said I would, but just for a few weeks. Those weeks turned into months. Still, Matt and I wrote love letters to each other and called when we could. We were still doing fine.

"Then Matt lost his job too. He came here to stay with Mona and me at our mama's house. A job came up at the high school for a math teacher. He took it. I found a good job too, managing a day care center. We went to estate sales and bought lovely things that we both adored." She made a wide, sweeping gesture that took in the whole apartment. "We even talked about buying a house in town. You see, we thought our luck was changing again. And it was—for the worse. Once we were settled in here, we started spending more time with my family. And some of the folks who thought I was too uppity to begin with started pulling Matt aside and telling him stories about how wild I was as a teenager. Sexually wild. Smoking dope. Things like that. The stories had some truth to them—I admitted that to Matt—but they were also greatly exaggerated. Matt said he didn't care. We even laughed over people talking about ancient history as if I was the first teen to rebel.

"But the truth is, deep down it set Matt up to believe that I was capable of almost anything. I'll never forget the day our relationship changed. It was at my mother's funeral, of all places. And Netty Lane pulled him aside—I saw them talking at the wake afterward—and I'm sure it was she who told him the lie. I'll never forget him staring at me, horrified, and her pointing at me. The next day he told me he was leaving me because he'd learned that I'd had an affair while I'd been here alone, away from him. I couldn't get him to admit that Netty

Lane was the one who'd told him—and of course she denied it too. But because of that, he left me."

If Matt had truly loved and trusted Mary, he'd have believed her, I thought—and then it struck me that I loved Hank but was all too quick to assume the worst when a female had answered his phone. And then I realized that Mary's situation was much like Sara Kirkland's had been. Sara had suffered from people gossiping about her husband's alleged affair; Mary had suffered from gossip about her behavior. I thought too of Netty's screaming obscenities at me when she realized I wasn't going to marry her son, calling me a whore and other similar names. Maybe that was how she saw any woman who refused to go along with what she and so many of her kinfolk saw as the only right and proper role for a woman.

I didn't point any of this out to Mary. I didn't see how these thoughts—however clarifying they were for me—could help her. Such observations would probably only make her feel worse. And of course I was eager for her to cut to the chase and tell me how she was going to help me find Bobby Lee.

But I didn't want to be too pushy and risk putting her off. "I'm sorry to hear that all of this has happened to you," I said. "I'm sure it's been a painful experience."

Mary nodded and stared into her glass.

"Why have you stayed here?" I asked softly.

She just shrugged. "I keep meaning to leave—maybe go back to Baton Rouge. I liked it there. Or start over in New Orleans or Atlanta. But I just can't seem to find the energy, somehow. Making it from day to day is hard enough." She sighed. "Matt's been gone for over a year now."

She was depressed, I thought. That's why she was letting herself stay stuck here instead of moving on and starting over.

Mary looked up at me and smiled, her eyes bright with wetness. "I'm sure you want to know what this has to do with you. Well, I hadn't spoken to Netty since Matt left. And I never thought I would. I got to thinking about what happened to you. There are some good people in the Lane family. But there are also plenty of them, like Netty, who'll do anything to manipulate things to fit their will, no matter who it hurts. I guess I saw an opportunity to get back at Netty—and even at Mona, who's been taunting me ever since Matt left that I wasn't woman enough to hold him.

"So yesterday evening, I went to call on Aunt Netty and Uncle Obediah. Told them I wanted to put bad times behind us."

I lifted my eyebrows at that. "And they believed you?"

"Of course," she said. "What I was telling them fit what they want to believe. They've always been like that, making up fantasies, then getting enraged when other people point out that actual reality doesn't always match their perception of it."

I thought about how Jimmy Joe had just made up our "love" for one another and had created his own version of me based on a few press clippings. I could see now, from what Mary was saying, where Jimmy Joe had gotten that trait. And what she said certainly matched my experience with the Lanes insisting that I must be wrong when I said I didn't want to marry Jimmy Joe, followed by Netty's hostile explosion when she realized I really didn't.

"Anyway," Mary went on, "I visited them and made up with them and then, when I got a chance, got into their spare bedroom." She rolled her eyes. "It's a virtual shrine to Jimmy Joe."

I shuddered at her confirmation of my earlier guess.

"I can tell you for sure that Jimmy Joe's been there to see them several times since his last escape—there's no way he'd miss seeing his parents, and they're too infirm to rendezvous with him out in the Okefenokee. And, to tell you the truth, given the area you'll need to search, I'm not convinced I'm helping you much. But I picked up a favorite childhood toy of his that he was sure to look at and touch whenever he visited."

"Won't it be missed?"

She shook her head. "Not for a while. It's always in a box in the bureau to keep it as preserved as possible."

Mary stood up, a bit unsteadily, and tottered into another room. Then she came back, bearing a brown grocery bag. She put the bag in my lap and then sat back down on her couch.

"I carried a huge handbag filled with crumpled newspapers so the bag already looked full when I visited. Then I swapped the newspapers for the item in the box. Go ahead. Look at it. I think it'll give you the scent object that you explained you needed when you called. And it might even provide some insight into Jimmy Joe."

I opened the bag, peeked in, and inhaled sharply. I had to close my eyes for a moment as waves of weakness, nausea, and dizziness came over me again.

In the bottom of the bag was a small, stuffed toy animal—a perfectly rendered bloodhound.

29
"Operation Recover Bobby Lee: The Search"
September 6, Friday, 3:15 P.M.

You don't have to do this alone," Hank said.

He was kneeling in front of me, making sure my voice wiring—which he'd insisted on in addition to the two-way radios—was perfectly adjusted.

"I know that," I said flatly.

Hank stood up. "I don't want you to do this alone," he said, emphasizing the word "want."

"I know that too," I said. I pulled up the top to my rescue suit and began zipping it. Normally, I'd give myself a few extra minutes out of the suit, especially on such a hot, humid afternoon, but I wasn't going to waste even a second today. Not for this search.

As soon as I'd finished my visit with Mary—it was all I could do to keep from running from her apartment with the stuffed toy in the bag, out of a sudden panicky fear she'd snatch the precious scent article back from me—I'd rushed home and called Hank. He'd come over immediately. We were in my office now. I had the search grid for around the Lane property rolled up and ready to go, not that I really needed it. I had memorized the area where I thought we'd surely find Jimmy Joe and Bobby Lee. Whenever I closed my eyes, that map danced behind my eyelids as if it had been emblazoned there.

Now, Hank gently took my chin in his hand and tilted my head up, causing me to look into his eyes.

"We could get Jasmine—you know she'd break off her mama vigil to go with you."

"No," I said.

"She'll never forgive you for not taking her with you."

"Yes, she will," I said. In many ways, she, more than anyone else, would understand why I wanted to do this alone.

"Another trainer?"

"No."

A long silence, as I gathered up the map and—very carefully—the now plastic-bagged stuffed bloodhound toy.

"I could go with you," Hank said softly.

"No," I said, smiling. "Hank, I've already agreed to extra precautions. When I find Jimmy Joe, if I go in with someone else, there's no telling what he might do to Bobby Lee." I shivered involuntarily at the thought. The chill of fear over Bobby Lee might keep the search suit from being unbearably hot, not that I was going to be giving much thought to personal comfort. "This is one search I have to do on my own. Alone."

I went to the door, but Hank stopped me again with his next words.

"Jo Beth, tell me that after this you'll never again go searching alone."

I knew he didn't just mean alone on a search-and-rescue mission. I said, "Hank, ask me after I've found Bobby Lee."

We drove to our designated starting point, about a half mile out from Jimmy Joe Lane's parents' house. I had Gulliver beside me. Hank and his deputy followed. The plan I'd agreed to was that I'd stay in contact via radio and wear the voice wire so they could pick up on my communication with Jimmy Joe, since I wouldn't want to use the walkie-talkie in front of him.

I'd also agreed not to subdue Jimmy Joe by myself, to keep providing coordinates based on the map and my compass, so that as soon as I did find Jimmy Joe, Hank would alert other authorities about my "unofficial" search and then the authorities would swoop in and recapture Jimmy Joe.

I agreed, thinking it was fine if it worked out that way. But if I had to break off communications for Bobby Lee's sake, I would. Rescuing him was my top priority.

And I'd also agreed to something else—that if I didn't have any success by an hour before nightfall, I'd cut off the search and return to base.

I'd agreed to that because I wanted Hank's cooperation in bringing the authorities down on Jimmy Joe, if possible. But I also knew something that I hadn't told Hank.

I wasn't coming out of the Okefenokee without Bobby Lee.

At base, we worked quickly, setting up the communications equipment.

Then, I carefully removed the scent article from the

large baggie to which I'd transferred it and held it out for Gulliver. His nose wriggled as he eagerly smelled the stuffed-toy bloodhound, taking in its scents. After returning the article to the baggie, I then gave Gulliver his signal that we were working—two pieces of dried deer jerky from my gloved hand.

"Seek, Gulliver!" I cried. "Find your man, find your man!"

Gulliver stared at me, playing the same waiting game for an extra serving of jerky that he'd played on our first search for Beulah Burton. I was prepared. This was no time to get into a contest of wills with Gulliver. I gave him the second handful of jerky. Gulliver began the jiggling dance that indicated he was ready to start the search.

I was ready too. Besides the scent article, I was backpacking a water bottle, a handgun and a rifle, a machete in case we had to go off trail in overgrown terrain, nutrition bars and more deer jerky, the transmission radio, flares, basic first-aid supplies, and of course the detailed map and a compass. I was starting first on a trail established by the Georgia Department of Wildlife for patrolling the area. The Okefenokee is a mix of plains and swamp, stretching thirty-eight miles north to south and twenty-five miles east to west. There was no way that I could cover every bit of it, although I was surely willing to try. But I hoped my theory was right—that Jimmy Joe used the few maintained paths that ran near his parents' house as a starting point to go off trail to a well-hidden shelter. I was counting on Gulliver to find Jimmy Joe's take-off point to his hiding spot—and lead me to Bobby Lee.

"Radio back in a few minutes," Hank hollered after me as I took off with Gulliver down the narrow trail-head.

I didn't reply or look back.

I kept track of our progress on my detail map and with the compass. We stopped periodically for water, calls of nature, sustenance.

All the little physical frustrations of searching that had bedeviled me in the past didn't even register with me this time. Sweat, bugs, exhaustion. I was numb to them all.

At first, the terrain was fairly level and easy going. As we delved deeper into the swamp, the ground rose and fell gently, and the brush grew thicker.

We worked our way around shallow, stagnant stands of water covered with green scum, keeping a fairly even pace. I kept a wary eye on the water, watching for the telltale parting of the green scum that would indicate an emerging alligator. I'd suffered an alligator attack once before on a search in the Okefenokee, and I didn't care to repeat the experience.

Every half hour, we found a cypress tree and took a break under its shade, for Gulliver's sake, not for mine. I felt I could go on forever, if I had to. But I could not afford to wear out Gulliver.

Now and then, I radioed back in to Hank, grateful that weather conditions were such that our transmissions were clear.

The sun began to set. I remained resolute, still only

resting to meet Gulliver's needs, continuing the search. Perhaps this would be my fate, to continue searching forever. So be it.

Hank radioed me, using the code name we'd established.

"Odysseus, this is home base calling. Odysseus, do you read me? Over."

"Home base, this is Odysseus. I read you, loud and clear. Over."

"Odysseus, this is home base. It's time to mark coordinates and return to base. Tomorrow's another day. Odysseus, do you read me? Over."

In response, I shut off the radio.

Before leaving home, I'd packed something in the bottom of my backpack, making sure that Hank hadn't seen it. Two flashlights, extra batteries.

Gulliver and I continued on, searching.

Twilight.

Gulliver, though growing weary, continued on.

Based on my map and my compass, we were now on a portion of trail that cut very close to the back of the Lane homestead—not even a quarter of a mile from their back door.

Discouragement seeped through me. This particular path would soon thin to nothing, and I'd have no choice but to backtrack and find another trailhead for another path. I found it hard to believe that Jimmy Joe would be this close to his parents' house because authorities looking for him routinely observed the house. Yet Gulliver had shown no characteristic excitement farther back on the path, and I couldn't believe that Gulliver had missed Jimmy Joe's scent.

What if the scent article was invalid? I'd trusted Mary, believed her, but it could be a cruel trick.

Gulliver's lead went taut. He was excited, moving faster. Soon I had to break into a trot to keep up with him. And then he stopped, suddenly, along the path, faced the tangled vines and undergrowth of the cypress trees. He breathed in raspily and erupted with his deep-throated bay.

Gulliver was signaling that he'd found his target!

No time to grab in the backpack for a flashlight. I plunged through the forest growth on pure faith, hanging on to Gulliver's lead with one hand while slapping vines and branches away from my face with the other.

Then, suddenly, we were in a clearing. Less than a hundred feet away, I saw in the last of the twilight the back of the Lanes's house.

The Lanes's house? Had Jimmy Joe been there all that time? It didn't seem possible, but there was nothing else in the clearing.

No. Gulliver was not leading me to the house, but to some specific spot in the clearing.

And then I saw where he was headed—and at the same time realized what had bothered me on previous visits that I hadn't quite been able to pinpoint—a discrepancy in the terrain that was so subtle and so unexpected it was easy to overlook. A slight mound of earth, covered in kudzu vines, abutted what looked like an old abandoned henhouse. But the vine-covered rise into which the henhouse leaned wasn't natural, and what's more, a thin trail of smoke was coming out of the rise through a barely visible pipe.

Gulliver wasted no time in pulling me over to the rise. He sniffed eagerly and on instinct I did something I hated to do but knew I must: I dropped to my knees and held Gulliver's mouth shut before he could bay again. He struggled, but I held on tightly, closing my eyes and letting the pieces fall together in my mind.

Once upon a time—and sometimes even now, because although legalized alcohol has cut into the moonshine trade, there are still "dry" counties—moonshiners built underground stills to hide their illegal art. A small tunnel, close to the surface because of the boggy land, would be built from the house to the underground still. The only exterior evidence of the underground still would be a ventilation pipe, necessary to let out smoke from the fire used to cook the mash, a mixture of sugar, yeast, water, malt, cornmeal, and sometimes other ungodly ingredients, such as lye, rubbing alcohol, paint thinner, bleach, or even embalming fluid, to give the result an extra kick. Kind of like the way Jimmy Joe's cousin had decided to give my drink an extra—and poisonous—"kick" by adding rubbing alcohol. Of course, moonshiners just wanted to make a profit, not poison or kill their customers, although that sometimes happened.

And this was an old underground still. The perfect hiding spot for Jimmy Joe. He could literally go to ground and still have perfect access to his mama and papa. And plumbing, home-cooked meals, and a phone to get in touch with his network of relatives—like Mona—who volunteered to keep track of me.

I opened my eyes and half-pulled, half-led Gulliver over to a cypress tree. He resisted mightily, and I knew I was preventing him from doing what nature intended him to do—bay that he'd found what I'd sent him to find, and stay by it. But if possible, I wanted the element of surprise on my side when I went down into that underground still.

I sharply commanded Gulliver to be silent and still. At first, he resisted, still wriggling, still trying to open his jaws. He was strong, certainly strong enough to break from me under normal circumstances, but these weren't normal circumstances. I was about to find Bobby Lee, I knew, and that gave me more strength than I'd ever had before.

In hissing tones, I repeated the commands to Gulliver until finally he submitted. I let go of him at last. Then I tied his lead securely to a cypress tree.

I didn't want to risk the sound of Hank on the radio, his voice possibly carrying to Jimmy Joe or his parents. So far, I'd seen no motion in the Lane house. Possibly they weren't home. Possibly I hadn't been spied yet. I turned my head to the left side of my chest where Hank had taped the voice wiring. Was he still listening for me?

"Home base, this is Odysseus. I've found Jimmy Joe," I said sotto voce. "He's hidden out in an underground still behind his parents' house. I believe the entrance to the still is through an old henhouse. Move in slowly and carefully. Gulliver is secured to a tree behind the Lane house."

I paused just a second before finishing with the words I knew Hank would hate to hear.

"I'm going in to the underground still. This is Odysseus, over and out."

I dropped to my knees, and began crawling toward the henhouse.

30
"Operation Recover Bobby Lee: The Rescue"
September 6, Friday, 8:00 P.M.

Although the old henhouse was swept clean, the place still held a faint smell of chicken shit. Now that I was inside the structure, I felt confident that the Lanes—if they were home—wouldn't be able to see me from their house. If only Gulliver would remain quiet, I would probably go undetected for a while, long enough to get inside the underground still and confront Jimmy Joe . . . and find Bobby Lee. I did not think about what I would do if I got inside and Bobby Lee was not there. The possibility was simply unbearable.

I slipped my backpack off as quietly as possible. Probably much of the floor of this henhouse was also the roof of the underground still and I surely didn't want to alert Jimmy Joe to an intruder's presence.

I felt in the bag and retrieved the flashlight. I decided against taking the walkie-talkie—the sight of a radio transmitter would alert Jimmy Joe to the fact that I wasn't entirely working alone. I picked up the smaller of the two guns, and felt its weight in my hand while I also weighed the possibilities. If I went in unarmed, how would I defend myself should Jimmy Joe get violent? But if I went in armed—and there was no way to conceal the gun in this jumpsuit, and in removing the jumpsuit I was sure to make noise that would alert Jimmy Joe—I faced the possibility that Jimmy Joe might overreact out of fear and harm Bobby Lee.

Also, with a gun, I faced the very real possibility that my anger with Jimmy Joe—surging now just below the surface of my calm, objective thoughts—would get the better of me and I'd shoot him on sight for having taken Bobby Lee. I'd been forced twice in my life to kill a man. I didn't relish a third killing and the inevitable guilt—no matter how justified or inevitable the killing might be—that would follow, along with torturous nightmares.

But what, a voice inside me murmured insidiously, if he's hurt Bobby Lee? What if you get inside and find Bobby Lee injured, maimed, neglected—or worse.

A cold answer snapped back. Then I won't need a gun to kill Jimmy Joe. Bare hands and fury would do.

I decided to leave the gun.

I picked up the flashlight, held its beam just an inch or so over the floor, so that its light only illuminated a few square inches and couldn't be seen outside the old henhouse. My aim was to find the trapdoor that would surely lead down to the underground still.

I moved slowly, feeling along the boards, thankful that they were relatively clean except for old bits of stray dust, some dried leaves that had blown in, and the occasional spider and mice droppings. Spiders and mice didn't bother me. And if a splinter rammed into my hand, I'd just have to hold back any yelp of pain.

I moved first along the walls, deciding I'd circle inward, forcing myself to go slowly, which now that I knew, deep in my heart, that I was only feet away from Bobby Lee, was very difficult. But I couldn't risk alarming Jimmy Joe that someone was coming in this way and have him scurry through the tunnel that I guessed connected the old underground still and his parents' house. I knew that if he ran, he'd take Bobby Lee with him.

For once, I got lucky. I only had to crawl three-fourths of the way around the interior perimeter of the henhouse before I found the old trapdoor.

I moved quietly to a crouching position. I put one hand on the iron ring that served as a handle to the door, while shining my flashlight on the door.

I got myself into a ready position, and counted backward from ten.

On one, I sprang into action: I pulled the door open, scurried to the edge of the hole, and dropped through.

I landed on my feet, upright, in a small, six-foot-high damp room that had been carved out of the earth and held steady by cinder blocks and cement.

Jimmy Joe stared at me from where he sat in an old chair next to a pile of still equipment, metal funnels and buckets. He was reading a Bible by the light of a kerosene lamp. To the left of the pile of old still junk was a small opening that gaped into darkness.

And there was Bobby Lee, lying on the floor next to Jimmy Joe. He was alive, and staring at me too.

I sank to my knees with a whimper.

Bobby Lee whined and tried to move to me, but he couldn't. A heavy chain was wrapped around his body and hooked to a heavy metal pot, the centerpiece of all the still junk. Bobby Lee had, at most, a two-foot range of motion.

I looked up at Jimmy Joe, anger mixing with my relief—and saw that in the few scant seconds I'd gazed at Bobby Lee, Jimmy Joe had pulled out a gun, which he was now training on me.

"Sorry about the chains around Bobby Lee," Jimmy Joe said. "He kept trying to get away from me. But I've tried to feed and water him regular like, and keep him clean."

I glanced at Bobby Lee, angrily slapping away tears that were coming to my eyes. Bobby Lee was clean, but I could tell he'd lost a few pounds.

"I'm sorry, ma'am," Jimmy Joe went on. "But you can't force a dog to eat. And I'm right sorry you got so sick. I just told Cousin Mona to give you a little bit of the rubbing alcohol. I think she must not like you because she went kind of overboard."

I glared at Jimmy Joe. "For someone who's willing to conspire to poison someone and kidnap her dog, you sure are full of sorries."

Jimmy Joe looked hurt, for all the world like a little boy whose hand's been slapped for wandering a few times too many to the cookie jar. I took a risk and decided to build on his vulnerability.

"And now you've got a gun trained on me. Is that any way to treat someone you say you love?"

"But you won't love me back," Jimmy Joe said, his

241

voice cracking the last word into two syllables. "And taking Bobby Lee was the only way I could think of to get you to me. Now that you're here, you can see I meant no harm to Bobby Lee." With his gun-free hand, Jimmy Joe reached over and scratched between Bobby Lee's ears. Bobby Lee whined and strained toward me. "So maybe we could get married after all?" Jimmy Joe added hopefully. "You'd only have to see me whenever I escaped from prison, so you could still run your business, and I'm sure I could get Mama to calm down and accept you, sooner or later."

I was exhausted. I was hurting. I just wanted Bobby Lee free. And I was angry. But somehow, Jimmy Joe's completely naive comments made me want to laugh. What was it Mary had said about her distant cousin and his parents? They made up whatever reality they wanted to be true.

"Jimmy Joe," I said, "don't you see you're not really in love with me? You don't know me at all. And if you did, you probably wouldn't like me all that much. I can be pretty bitchy, which is not what I think you want in a wife. It's not how your mama acts, is it?"

Except, I thought, when she was shrieking obscenities at any woman she considered a harlot. But I surely wasn't going to point that out.

A flicker of doubt crossed Jimmy Joe's face. "No, my mama knows her place by Pa's side. And that's the kind of wife I want."

"Well, Jimmy Joe, I hate to tell you this, but I'm a real women's libber. I don't think things would work out real well between us. I think you kind of decided what you want me to be like based on what you've read about me." Although, I thought, I couldn't imagine what he'd read about me that would give him any idea—even a basis for a fantasy—that I'd be a good choice for a traditional wife like his mama.

A faraway look came over Jimmy Joe's face. "I was going mostly by your picture. That and the fact you like dogs." He scratched Bobby Lee again. "Did I ever tell you I had a bloodhound as a kid?"

"I think you mentioned it," I said quietly. "But, Jimmy Joe, you have to admit that things just wouldn't work out between us, so why don't you—"

"But I also wanted that added to my ballad! About how I'd found the love of my life. There's nothing in my ballad about romance and there needs to be, a love all tragic because we're kept apart." Jimmy Joe's words came quickly, frantically.

My God. That was what this was about? His fantasy wife, based on my picture, and another verse for his ballad?

He was as far off in a fantasy world beyond reasoning as Sara Kirkland had been, and I remembered uncomfortably how I'd been able to get her to let her hostages go, but then she'd killed the two people she thought had hurt her before turning the gun on herself. Now, Jimmy Joe had a gun and he was essentially holding Bobby Lee and me hostage because the fantasy world he wanted wasn't coming true and, on some level, he knew that. I had failed in negotiating with Sara because I hadn't been able to reassure her that she'd get whatever it was she wanted. I had never even been quite able to figure out what she did want.

I couldn't fail this time, not if Bobby Lee and I were to survive. But at least this time I'd had a glimpse into the way Jimmy Joe perceived the world, and into what he wanted.

I licked my lips again. "Jimmy Joe," I said quietly. "Your ballad could have a verse about how you loved a beautiful lady and her bloodhound from afar." I had to be careful here, I knew. Ballads abound in which thwarted lovers kill their ladies. And Jimmy Joe was staring off with an otherworldly gaze. I wasn't sure if he even heard me—or if he did, what effect my suggestion was having. "About how . . . how . . . you both knew the beauty of a special bloodhound . . . and how through that bloodhound, you learned that your love was not meant to be."

Jimmy Joe stared off. I didn't dare glance at Bobby Lee because I knew I couldn't trust myself not to suddenly become hysterically angry and undo the progress I thought—I hoped—I was slowly making with Jimmy Joe.

I wondered if Hank was hearing any of this, if the authorities were rushing now to the Lane house to try to recapture Jimmy Joe. I hoped to God they didn't get here before Bobby Lee was freed and with me. I couldn't calculate what Jimmy Joe might do if he thought I'd tricked him so he'd be recaptured. But so far, I hadn't heard any sounds from outside that indicated movement or the arrival of reinforcements. I hadn't even heard poor Gulliver bay.

Suddenly, Jimmy Joe looked at me, tears in his eyes.

"Ma'am, that's just so beautiful. And it's true, isn't it? That'll make a good addition to my ballad." He nodded, satisfied.

But I couldn't be relieved yet. He was still holding the gun. And now he was looking at me appraisingly, the nonromantic, pragmatic aspect of Jimmy Joe kicking in.

"You didn't come alone, did you."

"Actually, yes, I did."

"But you're probably wired, or something."

I swallowed hard. Nodded slowly. "I'm not sure if I'm transmitting now or not, though," I said.

He sighed. "If I promise to leave you alone, will you promise not to search for me when I escape in the future?" He picked up the Bible he'd been reading, placed it on his lap, and put his gun-free hand on it.

I swallowed hard again, trying to guess what he wanted me to do. He pointed down at the Bible, then stared at me.

"Will you promise to leave both me and Bobby Lee alone, if I don't help search for you on future escapes?"

He nodded. Then he said, "But if you break your promise, I can't guarantee that I won't come after you. And your bloodhound."

I grinned—and Jimmy Joe showed good sense by recoiling at the sight, because my smile was everything but friendly. It was a warning. "And if you break your promise," I said, "I can guarantee I will come after you. And I'll make sure that when I find you, the material for the last verse of your ballad will be created."

Jimmy Joe Lane stared at me for a long minute . . . then smiled back, and nodded his understanding. I scooted forward, closing the few feet between us, took a deep breath, and put my hand on top of his on the Bible.

We didn't exactly exchange the vows his mama had hoped for, but we exchanged better ones. We'd leave each other alone henceforth. I'd get Bobby Lee—and my life—back. And Jimmy Joe would get his romantic verses added to his ballad.

After that, Jimmy Joe undid the complicated chain weavings that had held Bobby Lee in place for too long. Bobby Lee leaped toward me, and I held him, putting my face to his neck.

"Well, I'd better be going to see if they're out there for me or not," I heard Jimmy Joe say. Then I heard him start on his crawl through the tunnel to his parents' house.

But I didn't watch him go.

Instead, I held on to Bobby Lee, and sobbed in relief while he licked my face.

Epilogue
"And Finally, a Toast"
September 20, Friday, 7:00 P.M.

Nearly two weeks had passed since I'd finally found Bobby Lee. Jimmy Joe had crawled through the tunnel to his parents' empty house—they'd gone to a prayer meeting—and had walked out the back door and into the arms of the law. Hank had heard our entire conversation and had summoned backup, but had made all the officers wait quietly. I would forever be grateful to him for trusting me to handle the situation, because I still had nightmares about my final encounter with Jimmy Joe going much, much differently—nightmares in which in anger he shot Bobby Lee.

Now, Jimmy Joe was locked up again, and I figured it would be a long while before he made an escape attempt. He'd want "our" verse added to his ballad first. Still, I wasn't worried about him escaping. Maybe it was my taking a turn at believing in a reality I wanted to be true, but I trusted in our odd little promise to leave each other alone.

Tonight, twilight streaks of orange, red, and purple filled the sky, and I was happy to be doing nothing for the moment other than to stare at the colors from my favorite rocker on my porch. I stared intently, as if the colors would suddenly do something wild, maybe shoot off in all directions like some celestial fireworks show. Of course they wouldn't, and that was their beauty. Their only change was to soften into night; their magic, which kept me staring in fascination, was that in doing so, the colors somehow didn't lose their sense of power.

The day had been a scorcher. The air was still heavy and humid and warm, but I liked its feel, like an invisible comforting shawl. I held a glass of sweet tea, wet in my hand, and took a sip every now and then. The contrast of the cool liquid in my mouth with the warmth around me was also comforting, somehow.

Most comforting of all was Bobby Lee draped over my bare feet. He was snoozing, his paws twitching every now and again. What was he dreaming of? I wondered. Peaceful dreams, I told myself. Dreams of being on the trail with me, doing what he'd been born to do. Dreams, maybe, of chasing butterflies in a bright, sunny field. I loved the feel of his warm fur over my skin, but I kept staring at the twilight sky. I wondered how long it would be before I could look at Bobby Lee without a lump in my throat and my eyes tearing.

And tonight wasn't a night for tears. Jasmine and Susan were coming over for our usual Friday girls' night of pizza and beer and talk. I wondered too how much longer we'd have our Friday nights like this. I couldn't say change was in the wind—the air was as still and hunkered down as a rabbit in hiding. But somehow, I felt I could see change coming in those twilight streaks, sense it in the warm, humid stillness.

For tonight, though, I had plenty of bottles of beer cooling in the fridge, and Jasmine was bringing the pizza—sausage and onion and banana pepper—and Susan was bringing herself and, I sensed, some news. She'd sounded a little wary, a little careful when I'd called her earlier to make sure that she was joining us.

The sound of a car coming up the lane hooked my attention. I didn't stand up, partly because I didn't want to disturb Bobby Lee and partly because from the way Susan got out of her car and ambled up to my porch, she wanted to approach slowly, quietly, on her own terms.

The porch creaked from Susan's tread up the steps. She sat down in the rocker next to mine and began rocking. I took a sip of iced tea and waited.

"Pretty sky," she said finally.

"Yes." I didn't comment on the fact that she was twenty minutes early. Our girls' night wasn't officially supposed to start until seven-thirty. "Want some sweet tea?"

She laughed, softly. Carefully. "Nah. Looks like Bobby Lee is pretty happy right where he is. I wouldn't want you to disturb him."

I let a bit of silence spin out between us. "You know right where the sweet tea is, Susan," I said. "You know you can make yourself feel right at home."

More silence. "I know," she said. "Look, Jo Beth, I came a little early because I wanted to talk to you alone."

I looked over at her. "It's all right if Bobby Lee hears what you have to say, isn't it?"

Susan smiled, grateful for the light humor. "Sure. I, um, I just came from spending the afternoon with Leland Kirkland."

"I thought he'd gone back home."

"He had—but he's back down for a visit for the weekend."

"Worried about his parents?"

"Yes—but they're doing all right. He's really down to spend some time with me."

"I'm happy for you."

"I'm relieved, Jo Beth. I know you found him . . . attractive. I'm glad you're not upset."

I grinned. "He is attractive. And, like I said, I'm happy for you."

"He wanted me to tell you that things are working out great with Sherlock. That he understands your love of bloodhounds."

My grin widened. "Attractive and wise. Now I'm wildly happy for you. This means no more Brian Colby, I take it?"

"No more Brian Colby," Susan agreed with another quick laugh. "Or others of his ilk. I think Lee might be the right guy for me, Jo Beth. For keeps. I think I've finally figured out that a good man is hard to find."

"And a hard man is even better to find," I quipped.

We both laughed in the raucous way that defines our girls' nights, but when our laughter faded, there was an edgy silence between us again.

"That's not all you came early to tell me," I said. "Because I know you'll want to tell Jasmine too about your new relationship."

Bobby Lee gave a little snorting sigh, stood up, stretched his forelimbs. I gave him a long scratch behind the ears. Satisfied, he trotted over to Susan, and licked her calf, as if encouraging her.

Susan reached down, and scratched Bobby Lee some more. "Lee told me I needed to tell you what I told him." She took a deep breath, then stood up, pacing as she talked.

"You've always wanted to know who started the rumor about Leon and Norma Jean, who told me about their affair. The truth is, Sara herself told me her suspicions. I'm not sure what made her tell me. She just came into the Browse and Bargain one day, wanted me to help her find a book for Leon for a surprise gift, and as we were looking she ran across a baby-naming book, and next thing I knew, she was crying, telling me she thought Leon and Norma Jean were having an affair, and she didn't know what to do about it.

"It was bewildering. Sara had been in my store before, but she'd never wanted help in finding anything, barely said more than hello and good-bye to me on previous visits. But something about that baby-naming book made her open up. No one else was in the store, so I just listened and gave her tissues. When we heard the bell over the door tinkle, she suddenly got quiet and left without ever getting anything for Leon. It was like I'd dreamed it.

"Maybe that's what made me talk about it later—it was just so weird, totally unlike Sara. She was always so withdrawn, so tense. Anyway, I found myself telling someone about the incident—I don't even remember who now. I just—I just wasn't thinking. And then from there, all the rumors grew, and—and, oh, Jo Beth, I can't help but think that it was hearing all the talk that pushed Sara over the edge, that if she hadn't heard the talk, which I started, then maybe she wouldn't have, wouldn't have . . ."

I put my now empty glass on the small side table, then stood up, pausing for a moment to stretch. I'd been sitting too long. Then I caught Susan in midpace and pulled her to me. She leaned into me, crying openly now.

"What did Lee say when you told him this?"

Susan sniffled. "That there's no denying that betraying Sara's confidence in me was wrong. But that there was also no way to know if the talk was what sent her over the edge—or if something else would have sent her over anyway. He—he forgave me, Jo Beth."

I patted her back. "I do too."

"Thank you," she said.

We sat back down. "Lee told me that Leon had confided in him about the affair, so Sara's suspicions were right. Sara had had trouble trying to get pregnant, and she was getting obsessive about it, to the point that their marriage was falling apart."

"I reckon that explains why seeing the baby-naming book made her break down and confide her worries to you," I said.

"Yes," Susan agreed. "Lee also said he didn't think Leon was justified in using his marriage troubles as an excuse for an affair," she added quietly.

"Lee's right," I said. Then I added, with a grin, "See, Lee is a good man . . . and a good man is hard to find."

"And a hard man's even better to find," Susan returned, not even sniffling.

We laughed again, and this time our laughter lasted until Jasmine came up the porch steps. The heavenly scent of sausage, onion, and banana pepper pizza settled us down, although we were still giggling as we followed Jasmine into the house.

We ate in the kitchen, getting serious about the pizza and the cold beers. When there was nothing left but a few crusts and the take-out box, we had another round of beer. This silence was easy and satisfied, the kind that can only be shared by good, longtime friends.

I broke the silence first, looking at Jasmine and asking quietly, "How's your mama?"

I'd learned that Jasmine's mama had relented on the same night I'd found Bobby Lee, and had agreed to a long talk with her daughter. Jasmine hadn't shared any of the details, but I knew that since then she'd been visiting with her mama about twice a week, and that she'd been over at her mama's house before picking up the pizza for our girls' night.

"She's fine," Jasmine said, then grinned. "We're never going to be buddies. But we've at least made our peace."

Susan glanced over at me, then held up her beer bottle. "To making peace."

We all clinked our bottles together, then took a swig.

"Now," said Jasmine, "maybe one or the other of you can tell me what you were hooting and hollering about when I came up the steps."

I let Susan do the talking, telling as much as she was comfortable with, and I was glad that she cut out the part about her having started the talk about Leon and Norma Jean, and just stuck to gabbing happily about Lee and their blooming romance. We'd just toasted to making peace, after all.

When Susan finally took a break from talking, Jasmine held her beer bottle aloft again. "Here's to good men. And hard men!"

We clinked bottles, laughing. Then, midswig, Jasmine pointed at my left hand, and sputtered, "Oh, my God, Jo Beth. What's that? What's that?"

You'd have thought she'd spotted a snake curled around the ring finger of my left hand.

But it was just a simple ring, with a single emerald-cut diamond. I had kept the diamond turned palm-side down, until Jasmine had proposed her toast, and then had turned the diamond around so it could be seen more easily. Now seemed as good a time as any to share my—and Hank's—news.

"That, ladies," I said with more bravado than I actually felt, "is an engagement ring. Hank and I are getting married next month."

I tried to stay cool, I really did. I tried to let the nervous twitchiness that arose every so often ever since I'd said yes to his proposal a week before serve as the counterweight of reason to the giddiness Jasmine and Susan were displaying shamelessly at my news. I knew, after all, that ours would not always be a comfortable, easy marriage. We weren't suited for that kind of life. But, as Hank had put it when he proposed, we were better suited for rocky times together than smooth—but dull—times alone.

Jasmine and Susan got to me, though, and soon enough, I found myself laughing and giggling and jesting just as shamelessly as they were, while trying to explain that, no, the particulars of our wedding hadn't been worked out, and yes, they'd be very much in on the planning.

After a while, into the middle of our girls' night, Bobby Lee ambled in. We started cooing and fussing over him and minutes passed before I realized that I was actually interacting with Bobby Lee without getting teary eyed, for the first time since I'd reclaimed him.

As Susan and Jasmine went to get more beers, I stayed down on the floor, staring into Bobby Lee's big soulful eyes. And in his eyes I think I saw that all along I had been as much a searcher as he. For a sense of meaning, perhaps, or a sense of peace. And I realized that I'd finally found those things . . . with my bloodhounds, with my friends, with Hank, and within.

It had just taken a bloodhound to die for to show me the way.

Center Point Publishing
600 Brooks Road ● PO Box 1
Thorndike ME 04986-0001 USA

(207) 568-3717

US & Canada:
1 800 929-9108